"Don't assume anybody is harmless."

Sam was so close. Claire could feel the heat coming off his body. His lips were just inches away. And when his grip around her chin tightened, she knew he felt the connection as much as she did. Oh, man. Sam Vernelli shouldn't be worrying about her virtue or safety, he should be worrying about his own.

"I'm sorry," she said, pulling away. She couldn't think when he was touching her. "I got carried away at your expense."

He let his hand drop back into his lap. "You had me going," he admitted. "The watching thing was a little over the top. That's what did you in."

"Watching isn't your thing?" she asked, suddenly feeling bold.

He stared at her, not blinking, maybe not even breathing. "I prefer to participate...."

BEVERLY LONG

DEADLY FORCE

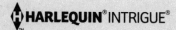

For Nick,
who has been a wonderful addition to our family!

Recycling programs
for this product may
not exist in your area.

ISBN-13: 978-0-373-69679-6

DEADLY FORCE

Printed in U.S.A.

www.Harlequin.com

ABOUT THE AUTHOR

As a child, Beverly Long used to take a flashlight to bed so that she could hide under the covers and read. Once a teenager, more often than not, the books she chose were romance novels. Now she gets to keep the light on as long as she wants, and there's always a romance novel on her nightstand. With both a bachelor's and a master's degree in business and more than twenty years of experience as a human resources director, she now enjoys the opportunity to write her own stories. She considers her books to be a great success if they compel the reader to stay up way past his or her bedtime.

Beverly loves to hear from readers. Visit www.beverlylong.com or like her at www.facebook.com/BeverlyLong.Romance.

Books by Beverly Long

HARLEQUIN INTRIGUE
1388—RUNNING FOR HER LIFE
1412—DEADLY FORCE**

**The Detectives

CAST OF CHARACTERS

Detective Sam Vernelli—Eleven years ago, he'd been madly in love with Tessa Fontaine and she was brutally attacked and killed. Now, he's prepared to do anything to save her younger sister, Claire Fontaine. But is he prepared to love again?

Claire Fontaine—With her life in danger, can she trust Sam Vernelli, a man she always believed was responsible for her sister's murder, to protect her? And will she finally accept that he's innocent?

Pete Mission—He's a talented coworker but does he have an ulterior motive when he offers to assist Claire?

Hannah Porter—She shares a cubicle at work with Claire. Are her questions as innocent as they seem or is she secretly jealous of Claire?

Sandy Bird—She's a stranger with a gun who barges into Claire's apartment. What possible connection could she have to Claire and why would she want to kill her?

Fletcher Bird—He's Sandy's husband and plays the role of the distraught spouse very convincingly. But does he know something that he's not telling?

Nadine Myers—She's been Claire's best friend since childhood. Does she know more than what she's saying about the intruder in their apartment?

Chapter One

Claire Fontaine sneaked a peek at her watch. Time hadn't stopped but it was moving pretty darn slowly.

"I've given this a lot of time and attention, people," her boss said. He stood at the head of the conference-room table, his arms flailing around as if they didn't belong to his body. His hair stood on end and there was a little speck of spit in the corner of his mouth.

"The new tagline for Smith Pharmaceuticals is 'When You Count Your Blessings, Count on Us.' We'll feature a modern family—a mom and dad both in business suits, three kids, all with smartphones, and lots of other technology in the background. We add an overlay, rolling across the screen, in old standard typewriter print. You know, High Blood Pressure, Type II Diabetes, High Cholesterol, Asthma. The contrast will be great. It'll hit home. No matter how things change, taking care of your family is what it's really about."

Claire looked around the table. Pete Mission, the most experienced designer, winked at her. Hannah, with whom she shared a cubicle wall, raised her auburn dyed eyebrows. They all knew it was her idea, knew that she'd been working even later than usual the last two weeks getting the idea into production.

But if her boss wanted to take credit, she didn't really care. She'd been lucky to get the job at Alexander and Pope. Not many advertising agencies were hiring and those that were all seemed to want at least five years of work experience.

Victor Santini beamed like a lighthouse. "Let's call it a night, people. We'll hit it hard again Monday." He pulled a rubber band off a stack of envelopes. "I've got your paychecks."

Nobody wasted any time. Claire reached for her check, folded the envelope and stuck it in her skirt pocket. She couldn't remember a Friday when Victor had let them escape early. Even if it was only twenty minutes, it was especially fortuitous because tonight she was going to confront Sam Vernelli.

Detective Vernelli. One of the city's finest. His picture had been in the paper a few weeks back. He and several other police officers had been honored at a luncheon and some reporter had decided that cops standing alongside the mayor was too good a photo op to pass.

It was terribly wrong that a man like him was responsible for enforcing the law. However, she wasn't naive enough to think she could change anything. The police hadn't been interested in what she'd had to say eleven years ago, so they certainly weren't going to be interested now. He was safe.

She just wanted him to know that there was somebody who knew the truth. Somebody who knew that he'd gotten away with murder.

Hurrying, she shut down her computer, packed it away, pulled her running shoes out of her shoulder bag and bent down to put them on. When she left the room, she opted for the seven flights of stairs instead of the elevator. Once outside, she walked fast and then waited impatiently for the do-not-walk signs at the busy intersections to flip over.

The mob of people on the sidewalk gradually thinned out as she left behind the commercial district and entered the residential streets, until finally after twenty minutes, she was the only one walking on the tree-lined sidewalk.

It was warm for late September and on any other day, the heat on her face, arms and bare legs would have felt good. But today, it made her hot and cranky and she was sweating and slightly out of breath when she reached Sam Vernelli's brownstone. She checked his house number against the crumpled-up slip of paper she clutched in her hand.

It had been ridiculously easy to find him. The internet was a wonderful thing.

She looked at the brick three-story that matched all the other brick three-stories that lined the quiet street. The houses were narrow and deep, but not as close together as she'd seen in some parts of the city. These people actually had yards.

There were three steps leading up to the front door. Mail had been delivered and envelopes peeked out of the metal box hanging on the side of the house. A big pot, with a sprawling gold mum that looked as if it needed watering, sat next to the solid-wood door. There was a huge tree in the front yard with leaves that were turning a deep red.

It looked normal. Nice.

Did his neighbors know that they lived next door to a killer?

Did they wander out in the evenings, intent on watering their small lawns, and end up making conversation with him? Did they invite him inside for a cup of hot chocolate after he helped them shovel snow? In a month, would their children trick-or-treat at his house?

Did his past matter to them? To his coworkers? To anyone but her?

It wasn't much, but at least tonight he would be reminded that somebody remembered. She'd intended to come that very same night after seeing the photo. However, when she'd gotten home from work, she'd quickly realized that her new flat-screen, some jewelry and half her underwear had been ripped off.

Welcome to the big city, country girl. At least neither she nor Nadine had been home. She'd filed a police report, gotten a bigger bolt lock and reminded Nadine of the importance of making sure it was locked when she left.

But now it was time to deal with unfinished business.

Sucking in a deep breath, she knocked on the door. Her heart was hammering in her chest, making it hard to breathe normally. She waited, then knocked again. Then a third time. She watched the curtains in the windows, looking for some telltale sign that he was home but unwilling to answer the door, but there was nothing.

She sank down on a step. She wasn't leaving. She owed Tessa this much at least.

SAM VERNELLI HAD BEEN working twelve-hour days for the past month and today had been no exception. However, because it was Friday, he'd agreed to go get burgers and beers with Cruz. His partner and best friend was still reeling from the fact that six months ago his wife had accepted a big promotion and moved to Texas, walking away from their six-year marriage.

Fridays had been date night for Meg and Cruz Montoya. And for the first several months after she left, Cruz got so damn drunk every Friday that he was still hungover Monday. Lately, he'd been better, but Sam knew he was a foothold away from slipping back into the mud.

Tonight, he and Cruz had both stopped at two beers. It might be the weekend, but they had an especially heavy caseload and they planned on working until at least noon Saturday.

Now, as he drove down his quiet street, all he wanted was a shower, a bed and at least eight hours of sleep. He slowed the car and eased it into an empty spot less than thirty yards from his house. He was grateful—sometimes by this time of night on-street parking was scarce. He could park in the alley, but that would mean beaching his car in front of his garage, which meant that he'd be blocking in Dolores. The woman had been a great tenant for the past three years since she and her adult son had rented both the third floor and his garage, but she also had the most annoying habit of going to the grocery store before the sun had fully crested the horizon.

He killed his lights. Just about to reach for the door handle, he caught something out of the corner of his eye. Streetlights made it easy enough to see that someone was sitting on his front steps.

It was a woman. Short, dark hair. Slim build. He couldn't see her face because her head was down, as she huddled over her bent knees. No coat, short sleeves. It was barely fifty degrees out—she had to be cold if she'd been there any length of time. There was a big purse or some kind of bag on the steps next to her.

She was no doubt waiting for Tom Ames. Dolores had mentioned he had a new girlfriend and this woman looked to be about the right age. But because he'd been a cop for a long time, he didn't see a need to be stupid. He quietly opened the door. He cut through his neighbor's yard, got to the alley and approached his property from the rear. It wasn't until he circled the entire house, making sure that nothing looked out of place, or that others weren't waiting in the shadows, that he approached the woman.

"Hello," he said and couldn't help smiling when she

jerked up and practically leaped off the steps. She was young, strikingly pretty, and while not exceptionally tall, she wore a skirt short enough that he still had a nice view of sexy legs.

Not a bad image to take to bed with him. And the next time he saw Tom Ames, he was going to yank his chain about leaving his girlfriend cooling her heels, or in this case, her tennis shoes on his front porch.

"Can I help you?" he asked.

She chewed on her bottom lip and Sam sensed the tension in her body. He moved slightly so that he could watch her for sudden movement and watch the street, as well. She stared at him, not blinking. He wasn't sure she was breathing.

"What's going on?" he asked, his tone still friendly.

The woman sucked in a deep breath and Sam was human enough that he appreciated the rise and fall of her full breasts under her lightweight shirt. But he was also very tired. "Look," he said, "let's cut to the chase. What are you—"

"Waiting. For. You."

Her voice was low, sexy, and he caught a sense of determined purpose in her carefully spaced cadence.

"Sweetheart, that's a nice thought, but you're a little young for me," he said. He felt bad when she flinched, but quite honestly, he didn't have the time or energy to play games.

"My name is Claire Fontaine."

The edges of Sam's vision went black. Tessa's little sister. On his porch. What the hell? It had been eleven years since he'd seen her. He did the math and realized that she was twenty-four. Days before this woman had turned thirteen, Tessa had dragged him to the post office, insisting that her little sister's gift needed to be there on her birthday. Three weeks later, he'd met Claire Fontaine when he'd gone to Tessa's funeral in Nebraska.

She'd been a skinny, dark-haired, dark-eyed teenager with a mouthful of braces who'd mostly stayed in her room. He hadn't paid much attention to her. He'd been too busy looking out the living-room window, staring at nothing, wondering how he was supposed to go on without Tessa.

Now that she'd given her name, he could see some resemblance to that young girl in the stunning woman who stood before him. The same dark eyes and dark hair, although it was shorter now, curling around her face. Slim, not skinny and there were definitely curves in all the right places.

"What… Why…" He stopped and took a breath. His interrogation tactics were generally better than this. No doubt about it. The woman had knocked him off-stride. "What are you doing in Chicago?" he asked, hoping he sounded more confident than he felt.

"Working."

The Fontaines had let another daughter move to Chicago? He could hardly believe that. "Where?"

"In advertising," she said, answering, yet not answering the question.

For some crazy reason, he felt stupid. As if he somehow should have sensed that Tessa's sister was close. In so many ways, he still felt connected to Tessa. He'd loved her and had been so sure they'd be together forever. And then she'd been killed and everything had changed.

He'd barely been back from the funeral when the cops investigating Tessa's murder had started looking in his direction. He'd been stricken with grief and suddenly facing the prospect of life in prison. It had been the most horrible time of his life.

And it was all because of this woman.

Claire Fontaine had told the police that she'd overheard Sam and Tessa arguing on the phone. Sam had threatened her sister, telling her she was going to pay for something she'd done. Just that quick, he'd become suspect number one. And because he'd found Tessa and gathered her cold body in his arms, his DNA had been everywhere.

Even as a dumb kid, he'd known he was in big trouble.

Even so, he hadn't done much to help himself. He'd been too busy crashing and burning and would have either died, too, or spent twenty to life in the joint if his parents hadn't stepped in. They'd spent money they didn't have and hired a big-name defense attorney who found plenty of holes in how the police had handled the investigation. Ultimately, the state's attorney had either realized that Sam was innocent or had figured he didn't have enough to take the case the whole way. For whatever reason, the man had declined to press charges.

Sam had started piecing his life back together. It hadn't been pretty and it hadn't been easy and even after he'd officially been discounted as a suspect, it had taken years before he'd been confident that he could go on. Now, in the seconds it had taken for her to say her name, the memories threatened to take him under.

What the hell was she doing here? "It seems to me that I'd be the last person you'd look up," he said.

She considered him. The light wasn't quite good enough to tell for sure, but he thought he caught the glimmer of unshed tears in her eyes. He refused to feel bad. She was the one who'd come from nowhere.

"How could you have become a cop?" Her voice was rich with unspoken accusation.

It wasn't the question he'd anticipated. He wouldn't tell her the truth. "I heard they had good pension benefits," he said. Sarcasm was always his backup plan.

She shook her head. "This was a mistake," she muttered.

She wasn't going to get an argument from him. Nothing good could come from his having anything to do with Claire Fontaine. And while he knew better, he couldn't stop himself from asking, "Why? Why now?"

Now the tears ran down her cheeks. "Because eleven years ago, I stood at my sister's grave and made her a promise."

She stopped, apparently unwilling to tell him what that promise had been. Hell, he'd made plenty of his own promises over the years. Not at Tessa's grave. His were generally silent oaths uttered to an empty room. And more times than not, a vodka bottle played a prominent role.

Even when he'd been sober, it wasn't as if he'd ever made good on any of them. Tessa's murderer had never been caught.

She reached for her shoulder bag. "I've hated you for a long time," she said.

He'd been a cop for eight years. She wasn't the first to say it. Never before, however, had the words clawed at his gut. "Look, your sister, she…"

He stopped. Tessa had loved her little sister, had always talked about how smart Claire was, how good of a student.

"What?" she challenged.

He shook his head. There was nothing, absolutely nothing, to be gained by going over ancient history.

"My sister was a beautiful woman, in the prime of her life." Her voice shook with emotion. "Not that I expect you to care," she added, her tone defiant. In a move that matched, she scrubbed the back of her hand across her face, destroying the evidence of her tears. She turned fast and practically ran down the steps.

Sam sank down onto the top step and rubbed the bridge of his nose. She was right. He didn't care. About much of anything. It was safer. Easier. And he sure as hell didn't need some ghost from his past reminding him why.

She was halfway down the block. *Let her go.* She'd come looking for a jerk, he shouldn't disappoint her.

"Hey. It's pretty late to be walking," he yelled.

She didn't even break pace.

Shaking his head, he jogged after her. And then she started running and he had to pour it on just to catch her. "Look," he said, grabbing her arm.

She swung her other one, aiming for his head.

He jumped back, both arms in the air, palms facing her. He was breathing hard. "I'll drive you home," he said.

"Get away from me," she said. There was enough illumination from porch lights and the occasional streetlight that he could see the anger in her dark eyes.

"You've got to be cold. At least let me call you a taxi."

"I don't want you doing anything for me," she said.

She started walking again and this time, he let her go. If the little fool got mugged, it wouldn't be his fault. He walked back toward his house. He was going to forget that she was in Chicago, forget her period.

When he reached his house, he saw the envelope lying in the flower bed next to his front steps. He picked it up and saw the return address of Alexander and Pope, one of the better-known downtown advertising agencies. It was a window-style, with her name and address clearly visible.

She lived in the 800 block of Maple Street. Her place was at least twelve blocks away. It'd be eleven, well past the time the crazies came out, by the time she got there.

I don't want you doing anything for me. He tapped the edge of the envelope against his hand.

Screw it.

He pulled his cell phone off the clip on his belt and dialed. "Squad, this is Detective 4433. Can you connect

me to a uniform in the vicinity of Maher and Oaktree?"
He waited impatiently for the call to be patched through.
When it was, he didn't waste any time.

"This is Detective Vernelli. There's a woman, dark hair,
early twenties, walking east on Oaktree, in the 2300 block.
She's headed to 810 Maple Street. Don't pick her up and
don't let her know you're following her, but call me when
she gets there."

When the officer agreed, Sam rattled off his cell number. Then he shut his phone, clipped it back on his belt and
very carefully folded the envelope. He'd throw a stamp on
it tomorrow and stick it in the mail.

He sure didn't plan on ever seeing Claire Fontaine again.

WHEN CLAIRE WOKE UP the next morning, her head ached,
her eyes were puffy and she was hungry. However, when
she reached for the skirt that she'd shed before crawling
into bed and realized that she'd somehow lost her paycheck, she felt truly ill.

How could she have been so careless? The last thing she
wanted to do was ask for a replacement check. She was still
proving herself at the job. What if the payroll department
happened to mention the request to her boss? It was a fast
slide down the corporate ladder when others thought you
were irresponsible. But it wasn't as if she could go without
a paycheck. She had her share of the rent to cover and although she'd already resolutely accepted that she was going
to be washing underwear more frequently, she hoped to
replace the missing television sooner than later. She was
a sucker for a sappy movie on a lazy Sunday afternoon.

She could have lost it anywhere between the office and
Sam Vernelli's house or between his house and her apartment. It had been dumb to stick it in her pocket when she
could have easily put it in her purse.

It was likely in Lake Michigan by now; they didn't call Chicago the Windy City for nothing. But it was possible that someone would find it and try to cash it. She'd have to tell someone so that the company could put a stop payment on it.

It was a perfect ending to a night where nothing had gone exactly the way she'd planned.

She'd sat on Sam Vernelli's steps for hours, getting colder and hungrier as the night wore on. She remembered closing her eyes and she must have fallen asleep. He'd scared the heck out of her when he'd suddenly appeared. Composure had vanished and suddenly it was as if she was thirteen again and her heart was racing as she sneaked into Tessa's bedroom at home to stare at the picture of Sam that was pinned to the bulletin board.

Back then she'd thought he was fabulously handsome. Now, eleven years later, his frame was more muscular, his dark hair shorter, and while his face showed some wear and tear, he was still very good-looking. In her world, he had the look that moved product, especially if women were the target audience.

He'd been shocked when she'd said her name. She'd wanted to throw him off balance. She just hadn't counted on the fact that her own equilibrium would be compromised.

He hadn't tried to convince her that she was wrong. Over the past weeks, once she'd decided that she was going to confront him, she'd spent time anticipating his response. She never figured he'd admit the truth. The man was a cop—he wouldn't be stupid enough to say that he'd murdered someone. No, she'd always assumed that he'd dismiss her accusations, maybe try to make her think she was crazy for thinking that she'd heard him threaten Tessa.

She hadn't expected him to just stand there and take it.

When he had, she'd expected to feel some sense of jubilation, but instead, all she'd felt was emptiness.

Going to see him had probably been a mistake. But she couldn't change it now. Thank goodness there were three million people in the city of Chicago. What were the chances she'd ever run into Sam Vernelli?

Chapter Two

Sam read while Cruz drove. He hoped the gritty details of the latest homicide would keep him from obsessing about Claire Fontaine.

She was different than Tessa and it wasn't just that her hair was dark and short while Tessa's had been blond and hung halfway down her back. No, it was something not quite so tangible. Tessa had been the life of the party, everybody loved her, especially men. While they were together, Sam had spent more than one sleepless night worrying about that. He'd always figured he'd been lucky to catch her.

Tessa had been...uncomplicated. He'd spent five minutes with Claire and somehow knew there was nothing simple or easy about her.

The radio crackled, blessedly interrupting his thoughts. "All units. District 23. We've got shots fired at 810 Maple."

Cruz grabbed the wheel with both hands. "We're four blocks from there. Want to go?"

Detectives, unlike uniforms, weren't required to respond to the all-unit calls. But neither Cruz nor Sam liked stuff happening in Area 5 that they didn't know about. "Sure. Let's roll."

Cruz whipped the car into traffic. "What was that address again?"

"810 Maple." As soon as he said it, Sam knew. He'd seen that address just the night before. "Drive faster," he said, as he pulled the envelope out of the inner pocket of his suit coat.

Apartment 3C. As Cruz weaved in and out of traffic, Sam tried to focus. Just because it was Claire's address, it didn't mean she was in trouble. There were probably lots of apartments in the building. But he couldn't shake the sick feeling that was in his gut.

By the time Cruz pulled up, police cars were stacked three deep. Sam grabbed his vest from the backseat and worked his way to the front. He slid in next to Bobby Horowitz, who crouched behind his vehicle, a phone to one ear, scribbling with a pen on paper that was balanced on his knee.

"What's going on?" Sam whispered.

Bobby held up a finger and Sam waited, sweat trickling down his back. Finally, Bobby hung up.

"Talk to me, Bobby."

"We got a report of shots fired. Neighbor across the hall called it in."

"What apartment?"

"3C." Bobby pointed toward the building. "It's that sliding door, third one from the left."

Sam leaned his head against the warm metal of the police car. He swallowed hard. "Any known injuries?"

Bobby shook his head. "Our guys got as far as the apartment door. They knocked and somebody started shooting. They grabbed the woman from across the hall and beat feet back down to the second floor. Ain't been a sound out of the apartment since then. Unfortunately, the neighbor hasn't shut up. She'd been going on and on about how the apartment was burglarized a couple weeks ago."

"What?"

"I don't know anything else. She didn't have many details. Hopefully, HBT will get here soon and we can put this one to bed."

Sam's stomach turned. Hostage Barricade Team. The last hostage rescue operation he'd worked, the hostage had ended up with a bullet in his neck. No doubt Bobby remembered it, too. He'd been standing next to Sam, looking like he wanted to rip somebody's head off.

Sam studied the building. It would be a long shot, but he thought he could do it. "Look, Bobby. From the balcony of the apartment next door, I can get over to that sliding door. The blinds are closed. They aren't going to be able to see me from inside."

"So, then what?"

"It's been warm this week. I'm betting they open that sliding door. Because they're on the third floor, they probably keep it unlocked."

"I don't know. You fall three stories and it's my job."

"I get them out of there and it's the mayor calling you up, inviting you over for drinks."

Bobby's green eyes took on a familiar glow. "Yeah, I'd like that. Maybe the guys from HBT could drive me there." He looked at his watch. "Get going. Super said every apartment is laid out the same. Railcar-style. That sliding door is to a bedroom, which connects to another bedroom, then there's the living room, kitchen and finally the bath."

"Make sure our guys on the second floor know I'm coming in," Sam said, moving fast. He slipped inside the building, his gun drawn. When he got to the third floor, he stopped, listened and then moved toward the door he needed. He unlocked it and went inside. He listened again but didn't hear anything from Claire's apartment.

That didn't necessarily mean good news.

He walked out onto the balcony, staying close to the

building. After attaching the radio to his belt, he slipped his gun into his shoulder holster and inspected the bricks. He pushed his fingers in between them, hoping to get some kind of hold. It wasn't much but it did provide some balance. He stepped up onto the wrought-iron railing, first one foot and then the other.

Then he made the mistake of looking down.

His heart thumped. One good jump, he reminded himself.

Right. If the first one wasn't good, he wouldn't need to worry about a second try.

Sam took a breath and closed his eyes. From inside the building, from Claire's apartment, he heard a scream and then a gunshot.

Sam opened his eyes, bunched up his leg muscles and leaped. He hit the deck with a soft thud, his knees absorbing the shock. He yanked on the door handle and started to breathe again when it slid open. Easing his hand inside, he caught the edge of the heavy curtain and pulled.

He poked his head and gun through the opening. Empty. It was a mess, with clothes and shoes everywhere. He moved quickly, his shoes making no sound on the carpet. Through the door, into the interior bedroom

It smelled like Claire Fontaine. Fresh with a hint of something exotic. Everything in its place. The bed covers were thrown back, as if someone had been sleeping.

He poked his head out the door and scanned the living room. His stomach cramped up tight.

A woman, half her head blown off, lay sprawled on the couch. Blood and tissue splattered the wall behind her. She was blond and many pounds overweight—not that she was going to need to worry about that anymore. A cigarette, still smoldering, rested in a butt-filled glass dish on the end table.

Across from her, a young woman, red hair, very pale skin, wearing standard-issue green scrubs, sat on a love seat. A revolver rested in the palm of her hand. She had her eyes closed but he didn't think she was hurt. He could see the rise and fall of her chest, in even breaths.

Where was Claire?

Sam focused on the woman in scrubs because the woman on the couch wouldn't ever be moving again. He slipped behind her. "I'm a police officer," he said, keeping his voice soft. "Put your gun on the floor."

She strained her neck to see him. Her eyes were open, her stare blank. She looked first at the gun he pointed at her, and then back at her own gun. Without a word, she bent over and gently placed it on the floor, next to her bare feet. Sam walked around the end of the couch, squatted, picked up the gun with his fingertips and dropped it in the pocket of his suit coat.

"Where's Claire?" he asked.

"I'm here."

Sam whirled around. Claire was at the far end of the apartment, leaning against the frame of the bathroom door, so pale that he wondered how she could stand. She had a hand towel up to her mouth.

"Anybody else here?" he asked, trying to stay focused. He could see streaks of tears on her cheeks.

She shook her head and made the mistake of looking at the dead woman. She swayed, her shoulder knocking into the wall.

He moved quickly to her side and wrapped an arm around her shoulder, pulling her in close. Her whole body was trembling. "Are you hurt?" he asked.

She shook her head.

"You're sure?"

He got a nod. Okay. Sam pulled back a little. Claire's

eyes were puffy, her nose was red and she kept the towel up to her mouth, like she wasn't sure she was done losing her lunch.

"Who's that?" he asked, nodding his head toward the woman in scrubs.

"My roommate, Nadine."

"Okay. Look, I need to call this in," he said. "Nadine, come over here. I want the two of you to sit in the kitchen."

He led Claire over, keeping one arm around her. He kicked a pair of green rubber clogs out of the way and used his free arm to pull two kitchen chairs away from the table. He faced them toward the kitchen counters.

He lowered Claire down and backed away when he was sure she was steady. Nadine took the other seat without a word.

He pulled the radio off his belt. "Squad, this is 4433. I'm inside at 810 Maple. Let all units know the location is secure and roll me an ambulance."

CLAIRE FOLDED THE WRAPPER over her half-eaten cheeseburger and pushed the almost-full container of fries toward the middle of the table. "I'm done."

"At least you ate something." Sam Vernelli gathered up his own garbage, added it to hers and put it on a tray that he shoved to the end of the table.

"I…" She stopped, pressing two fingers hard against her lips. "I've just never seen anything so horrible before."

"There are cops who've been on the job for ten years who haven't seen anything like that. It would shake anybody up."

He was being nice and kind. The same as he'd been since he'd somehow, like some superhero, jumped onto her balcony. It was one more crazy thing in a day of craziness.

For the last eleven years, Sam Vernelli's name had been

synonymous with everything evil. She didn't want him to be nice to her. She didn't want to owe him anything. But when he'd pulled her into the kitchen and squatted in front of her, his hand steady on her knees and his eyes even steadier, it had been hard to remember that.

And suddenly it had seemed as if there were a hundred people in her apartment. Cops who wanted to talk to her, then to Nadine, then to both of them. The paramedics from the ambulance had arrived, looked at the dead woman and left. Then some skinny guy, who everyone called The Weasel, in a black suit that looked too big for him had walked around with a camera and if he'd taken one picture, he'd taken a hundred. Of everything, from every angle.

And when it had been over and she'd been so light-headed that she thought she might faint, she hadn't protested when Sam had practically dragged her out of the apartment and across the street to McDonald's. She'd been a quivering mess.

It was time to suck it up. "I need to go."

Sam looked at his watch. "It's not quite four yet. I've got a few more questions."

"Look, Detective Vernelli, you and I both know that it's not a good idea for you to be assigned to this case."

"It's a little too late for that."

"No. I'm going to call the police department and request that another officer be assigned."

Sam pulled a card out of his pocket. He wrote down a name and number and shoved it toward her. "This is my boss's name and cell. Right about now, he's walking his daughter down the aisle, so I don't think he'd appreciate the interruption. But on Monday morning, you can call him. Make your request. I don't really care. But for now, I've got a dead woman and a hell of a lot of unanswered questions. I'll do my best to stay out of your way, but I'm not going to sacrifice this investigation just because you've got a problem with me."

Claire chewed on her lip. "All right, fine. But don't think I won't call Monday."

He shrugged. "I'm counting on it. Now, start at the beginning."

She'd never wanted to do anything less, but just maybe, if she went through it again, it would start to make some sense to her, too. "I got up pretty early this morning. I was mad at myself because I'd somehow managed to lose my paycheck last night."

Sam held up a finger and reached into the inside pocket of his suit jacket. "I found this next to my steps."

She grabbed the envelope. "Thank you. One less thing to have to deal with on Monday."

"So you got up early…" he prompted.

"Yes. I realized Nadine was still sleeping, so I quietly made some breakfast and then went back to my bedroom. I had left a couple projects undone at work, so I figured I'd use the time to catch up. I worked for a few hours on my laptop. I got a little sleepy and decided to catch a nap. When I woke up around eleven, I heard voices in the living room. I recognized Nadine's voice, so I walked out to see what was going on. She was telling the stranger to get the hell out of our apartment."

Sam flipped the pages of his notebook. "Nadine said that she was leaving for work and the woman had been in the hallway when she opened the door. She'd pushed her way into the apartment."

Claire shook her head. "What kind of crazy person does that?"

Sam shrugged his broad shoulders. "I don't know. What happened next?"

"The woman pulled a gun out of her pocket and started

waving it around, screaming. It was pretty disjointed. Something about everything was ruined and that she wasn't going to be the last fool left standing. She pointed the gun at us and she was shaking so much that I was afraid it was going to go off. She told us to sit down and when we didn't move fast enough, she shot the gun. The bullet went over our heads, probably just a foot or two."

"That's probably what saved your life. The neighbor across the hall heard it."

"Mrs. Peters. She hears everything."

He smiled and she realized it was the first time she'd seen him do that. His teeth were white and straight and he looked like some model on the cover of *GQ*. She remembered overhearing her mother tell one of her friends that Sam was as handsome as Tessa was beautiful.

She swallowed hard and focused on getting the details right. "Nadine and I sat on the love seat and the woman sat across from us on the couch. She got really quiet. Then the police knocked on the door. She went crazy again and shot twice at the door."

"Then what?"

"She was smoking one cigarette after another. Every once in a while, she'd wave her gun around. She asked us how much money we had and I told her I had sixty dollars in my purse and Nadine said she had about two hundred."

"What did she say?"

"She started laughing hysterically, and said that wasn't nearly enough. That she couldn't have any kind of life on that kind of money. Then she pointed the gun at us, said she was going to have to kill us after all, and I knew she meant it."

"But Nadine shot her first?"

"Yes. I just sat there and waited to die. Nadine, thankfully, wasn't quite so willing to give up. Her backpack was wedged between the two seat cushions. When the woman was ranting, she somehow managed to reach into it, pull out a gun and shoot her."

"And you said earlier that you had no idea that she had a gun."

She shook her head. "No. She had mentioned something about a woman getting attacked in the parking lot at her work and that she was thinking about getting a gun. I didn't realize that she'd followed through on it. I've never been all that crazy about guns, but call me a hypocrite because right now, I'm pretty darn glad she had it."

Sam smiled. He glanced through the pages of his note-book again before looking up. "And neither of you ever met this woman before?"

"No."

Sam rubbed his jaw. "Not through your jobs? Not some night at a bar?"

"No." She pushed her empty soda container to the center of the table. "She was a stranger. I don't even know her name and now she's dead."

"Her name is Sandy Bird. Ring a bell?"

"Sandy Bird," Claire repeated. She let the name roll around in her head but it didn't bump into anything familiar. "How do you know that's her name?" she asked. "That's pretty fast police work."

He shrugged, letting her know that her grudging admission hadn't been lost on him. "It wasn't all that tough. She didn't have a purse or a wallet on her, but she did have a set of keys in her pocket. When you were talking to the others, I walked outside, pointed the electric door opener at several cars, and sure enough, the lights on the green Toyota Camry started blinking. Her purse was in the trunk and when I matched up the license picture with uh...her face, I knew it was her."

"She doesn't have all that much of a face left," Claire said, swallowing hard.

"A family member will need to make a positive ID down at the morgue. My partner, Cruz Montoya, is helping the coroner chase that down right now." Sam pulled his straw out of his empty container and started tapping it on the table. "I understand your apartment was burglarized just a few weeks ago. Do you think this has anything to do with that?"

"I have no idea."

He bent his straw double, then again, until it was a hard ball of plastic. He relaxed his hold and it sprang apart. Then he started folding again. "How long have you known Nadine?"

"Forever. We went to grade school together. We'd been planning this move to Chicago all through college. We both took jobs in Omaha after graduation. I needed some work experience before advertising agencies in Chicago would consider me. When I got the job at Alexander and Pope, she applied for nursing positions. She got one at Melrey." Claire scooted to the edge of the booth. "Look, if there aren't any more questions, I'd like to go."

"Your apartment is a crime scene. You can't stay there."

Right now, she didn't ever want to see her apartment again. "I know. I can't even have it cleaned up until I get the okay. Fortunately, one of the officers gave me a business card. He said they'd do a good job."

Sam shook his head. "They aren't supposed to do that. Just so you know, it's probably his cousin."

She shrugged. She couldn't care less. Their landlord had been one of the hundred people who'd flooded the apartment. He'd told them it was their responsibility to get the apartment cleaned and repainted. She and Nadine had agreed the couch was simply getting thrown out.

"So where are you two planning to stay?" he prompted.

"I'm staying at a hotel." At the cheapest one she could find. Her credit card balances were mounting. "Nadine's going home for a week or two. She worked it out with her supervisor."

"I'm not crazy about her leaving right now," Sam said. "I might have more questions for her."

"I have her cell number, her mother's cell and her parents' home number." Claire slid her purse strap onto her shoulder. It wasn't going to be Sam Vernelli's worry. She was making that call at eight o'clock Monday morning.

He pointed to his card that was still clenched in her fingers. "My work number is on that card. Let me give you my cell, in the event that you think of something else or if you…need anything."

"Do you give your personal cell number to all your crime victims?" she asked.

"You're not just anybody. You're Tessa's—"

"Little sister." She squared her shoulders. "I don't think either one of us can forget that." She squatted and reached for the handle of the black duffel bag that she'd stuffed under the table. "Good night, Detective Vernelli."

"I'll drive you to your hotel."

She shook her head.

He looked as if he wanted to spit nails. "Fine. I'll get you a cab."

She held up a finger. "Detective Vernelli, I am grateful for your assistance today. To say I wasn't would be lying. But you and I both know that nothing good can come out of our having anything to do with one another. So, don't call me a cab. Don't call me period."

Chapter Three

Sam dialed Cruz's cell as he walked to his car. When Cruz answered, Sam asked, "Hey, can you talk?"

"Yeah," his partner said. "It's just me and a couple cheeseburgers sitting in my car. I thought you and Claire were grabbing a bite."

"Yeah, well, she eats fast. So what do we know about Sandy Bird?"

"She's got two kids, ten-year-old twins. She's the president of the Arlington Heights Parent-Teacher Organization."

"None of that makes any sense. What would she be doing breaking into an apartment on Maple? Is she married?"

"Yes. For the last ten years. To Fletcher Bird. He's a pharmacist, works in the Loop."

"What's your read on him?" Sam asked.

"He's shook, doesn't know what to tell his kids. Said that he had no idea why his wife would have been in Claire's apartment. The names Claire Fontaine and Nadine Myer didn't mean anything to him."

Sam closed his eyes. Nothing was ever easy. "Okay. You want to start the process for us to check the phone and computer records?"

"Request is already in. He and his wife both had a cell

and a home phone. PCs at home and his office. Claire has a laptop and she and Nadine each have a cell and one landline. You know, this used to be easier before everyone needed to be connected 24/7."

"I know." Sam wondered if Claire had any idea that her privacy was about to be compromised. "I had The Weasel snap pictures of both Nadine and Claire. I don't want to push the husband too hard when he's got his hands full of funeral arrangements, but I think we need to see if he recognizes either of them."

"Maybe she just picked today to go off the deep end," Cruz suggested. "Maybe her husband's name finally drove her over the edge. By the way, I pulled the full robbery report. I was going to call you but I didn't know if you'd want to be interrupted." His tone was full of suggestion.

Sam started his car and pulled out into the heavy traffic. "I told you, she's Tessa's sister." Cruz and his boss were the only two in the department who knew the story. "We grabbed a bite to eat and she's on her way to a hotel." No need to add that she'd done it without a backward glance in his direction.

"She's a beautiful woman. Nobody was questioning why you decided to leap tall buildings to save her."

Sam sighed. "I was doing my job, Cruz."

"Half the guys trooping through her apartment today plan to ask her out. The other half are either gay or too afraid she'll shut them down and they'll never recover from the pain."

"That's ridiculous. She's only twenty-four."

"Last time I checked that was six years past legal."

Sam switched lanes quickly and horns blared in response. Yeah, so what that he'd noticed that she looked really good in her black leggings and long sweater that was snug in just the right places? He was human, wasn't he?

Debatable. At least from Claire's perspective. She'd made it pretty clear that she wasn't impressed and no doubt would make her call first thing Monday morning.

The case would be reassigned and he'd be out from under this rock. Good.

ON SUNDAY MORNING, Cruz bumped his leg against Sam's desk, carrying a stack of manila folders, two large coffees and a white sack. Sam reached for the coffees and Cruz dropped the folders on the desk. "So much for Sunday being the day of rest," Cruz said. Then he opened the sack and pulled out some kind of egg and sausage thing on a biscuit with cheese dripping over the side.

"You used to eat cereal and bananas in the mornings," Sam said.

"That's what Meg liked for breakfast."

He could let it pass. He probably should. "Here's a news flash, Cruz. It's your arteries that are getting clogged. When you eat that stuff, you're not hurting her."

Cruz pulled a file from the stack. "Practice your amateur psychology on somebody else," he said. He flipped the file onto Sam's desk. "The report on the robbery at Claire's apartment is on top."

Sam opened the file and skimmed over the information. When he got to the list of items taken, he slowed down. One flat-screen television. Three necklaces. One ring. Approximately ten pairs of panties. He raised his gaze and looked at Cruz. "Did you read this?"

Cruz nodded. "I don't remember Claire mentioning the panties yesterday."

Sam shook his head. "No. I'm pretty sure Sandy Bird and Claire wouldn't wear the same size."

"You're right. I called the morgue this morning and they checked her personal items. White cotton, size eight.

Claire's were a size five. And truthfully, Claire doesn't look like a white cotton girl to me."

Neither one of them had any business thinking about Claire's underwear. "Did they get any prints from Claire's apartment?"

"There was one set of prints that didn't belong to Nadine or Claire. They aren't Sandy's either. So, A, if Sandy was the thief, she was careful and wore her gloves like a good girl. Or B, the prints belong to the thief, but he's a new thief with no record. Or C, the prints belong to some jerk they had over for beers one night who had nothing to do with the robbery. Basically, we don't know squat, except that the thief likes women's underwear."

The thought of some sick idiot running his hands over Claire's stolen panties made Sam think his coffee might make a return appearance. He swallowed hard and focused.

"Eat fast. We need to go talk to Sandy Bird's neighbors. If we're lucky, we'll get to the people who work at the drugstore by early afternoon."

A half hour later, they were walking down Sandy and Fletcher Bird's street. It was edged with trees, just blocks away from the train line that ran through downtown Arlington Heights. The houses were two-stories, there was an abundance of swing sets and the neighbors were naturally curious.

They had known Sandy and liked her. At the third house, the one directly across the street, Sam and Cruz heard something interesting from the thirty-something woman who answered the door with a toddler on her hip.

"Sandy and I used to go to the gambling boat. It was a quick twenty-minute drive. And the buffet was delicious."

Sam almost laughed. Of course. The slot machines had nothing to do with it.

"How often did you go?" Cruz asked.

"Once a month, maybe. We'd get a sitter for the kids. It was fun."

And probably pretty harmless unless she was losing big. "What's the most you ever saw her lose?"

The woman shrugged. "Maybe a hundred dollars."

A hundred bucks a month? Didn't seem like much of a gambling problem. But Sam recalled what Claire had told him. *She wanted to know how much money we had.*

"Do you think she ever went by herself or with another neighbor?"

"I don't think so. She was pretty busy with her kids. Fletcher worked a lot of hours and was gone a lot."

They thanked her for the information and left. Three houses later, the consensus was that Sandy Bird was a good mom, a willing volunteer and a poor golfer. None of that helped them understand why she'd stormed her way into a stranger's apartment and started shooting up the place. They did not go to see Fletcher Bird. His car was in the driveway, but they kept their distance out of respect. There'd be time to talk with him later.

They headed back downtown, toward the South Loop. Because it was Sunday, and the office buildings were mostly empty, they had no trouble finding a place to park right in front of the drugstore.

They flashed pictures of Nadine and Claire. All three of the clerks, all women in their forties or fifties, shook their heads. *Pretty girl,* said one woman, pointing to Claire's picture.

Flat-out beautiful, really, Sam thought. Voluptuous. Not stick-skinny like so many women aspired to be. A man wouldn't lose her in the sheets.

He stopped walking so suddenly that Cruz almost ran into the back of him.

"What?" Cruz asked.

"Nothing." He waved a hand. "Let's go."

What the hell was he doing thinking about Claire Fontaine wrapped up in nothing but a silk sheet?

ON MONDAY MORNING, before Claire had a chance to stuff her purse in her desk drawer, Victor's secretary was knocking on their cubicles, letting the creative staff know that Victor wanted to see them—post haste.

The buzz immediately started. Finalists for the Chicago Advertising Association's Design of the Year contest were supposed to be announced today. Victor was the contact for all the entries. Was it possible that one of them had been nominated as a finalist?

"What's this about?" she heard Pete Mission ask.

Juanita, who, just the week before, had roared past sixty without blinking an eye, sighed. "Who knows? For having a degree in communications, he doesn't share much. All I know is that he's been pacing around his office like a little kid waiting for Christmas."

Claire and the others took the elevator from the seventh floor to the ninth floor, where all the executives had corner offices. One by one, they filed into the conference room and took their respective chairs. There were no name plates or assigned seats, but still, everybody had a spot. And if somebody tried to shake things up by taking a different chair, no one was very happy. Several had brought work with them. Others were just content to let their brains relax. They were prepared to wait. Victor hadn't started a staff meeting on time since the beginning of staff meetings. There had been lots of jokes that he couldn't actually tell time.

They almost fell over when Victor arrived within minutes. His cheeks were pink and his small eyes were bright.

He was smiling. It was the first time Claire had ever seen him happy.

He didn't waste any time. "We were notified this morning that two of our entries are finalists in this year's contest."

Two. Wow. The competition was incredible. If an agency had one finalist, they were generally ecstatic. Even the more nonchalant staff members were sitting up straight in their chairs.

"I'm delighted to share that both Pete Mission and Claire Fontaine will be competing for this year's grand prize."

Oh, my God. She'd only been at Alexander and Pope two weeks when the memo went around, encouraging everyone on the creative staff to get their entry completed and submitted. She'd reviewed the guidelines and worked like a crazy person to develop something.

Hannah stood up and pumped her arm in the air. "Two. Amazing. Congratulations, Pete and Claire."

Everyone clapped and cheered. At least Claire thought it was clapping and cheering. Maybe it was just her heart clanging in her chest. She made eye contact with Pete. Even he looked stunned.

Victor held up his index finger, attempting to bring order to the room. "Their designs will compete against the other four finalists. The committee will announce the winners exactly one week from today at the awards dinner. This is big, people, really big."

As they filed out of the room, there were more private congratulations. Claire looked for Pete to offer her congratulations to him, but he was gone.

"Where's Pete?" she asked Hannah.

The woman shrugged. "Probably out arranging for a

tux and a limo. He's entered for ten years straight and this is the first time he's been a finalist."

Ten minutes later, Hannah was still hanging over the cubical wall that Claire shared with her. She was speculating on what Claire should wear to the awards dinner. Claire's telephone rang and she reached for it, grateful for the interruption. Hannah smiled at her, before her face disappeared from view.

"Claire Fontaine."

"Hi, it's Sam Vernelli."

Like she wouldn't have recognized his voice. She cupped her hand around her phone, attempting to create some privacy. Hannah out of sight didn't necessarily mean Hannah out of hearing. "Detective?" she said, her voice low.

"How's it going?" Sam asked.

"I just…" She stopped. She couldn't tell him about the contest, about how absolutely psyched she was about being a finalist. That was something you told a friend, a confidant. He was neither.

"You just what?" he prompted.

"Nothing. What can I do for you?" she asked, her tone purposefully brisk, businesslike.

"I wanted you to know that we're releasing the scene. You can get your apartment cleaned up."

She pictured the splattered wall and swallowed hard, suddenly glad that she'd skipped breakfast. "I'll call the painter now. Maybe I can have him meet me there tonight." She really didn't want to return to her apartment, but unless she planned on living indefinitely in a hotel, she needed to do it. She needed to put the ghosts behind her.

All night, she'd tossed and turned, wondering about the woman, reliving every word she'd said. At about two, she'd given up all pretense of sleeping, booted up her laptop and forced herself to work on upcoming proposals.

The work was bad and would need to be redone, but it beat dreaming about dead women and blood-spattered walls any day. She kept thinking about the woman's family. "Did you talk with Mr. Bird?"

"Briefly and only on the phone. He's busy planning a funeral. I gather that he's pretty worried about how his boys are going to handle this—they're just ten."

Three years younger than she'd been when she'd faced death for the first time. She'd lost her sister before she'd ever really known her.

When Tessa had left Nebraska at eighteen to go to college in Chicago, Claire had been in fifth grade. She'd been more interested in computer games and birthday parties than in establishing a relationship with her sister.

She barely remembered the funeral. It had been a crazy couple of days. People in and out, calls to and from the police in Chicago, trips back and forth to the airport to pick up relatives. Death was a noisy affair.

Then, when all the people had left, the house had gotten quiet, very quiet. She'd been too young to understand it then. It was only later that she realized that everyone had been drowning in grief. Tessa's death had stripped the sunshine out of their lives, leaving behind a cold, unforgiving torrent of rain.

And as hard as she'd tried, as good as she'd been, she'd never been able to make her parents smile in quite the same way again.

"Is there anything else, Detective?" she asked, her throat feeling tight.

"We'll continue to investigate—probably talk to a few neighbors and check out the drugstore where Fletcher Bird works. I'll call you if I have any more questions."

"That's…fine. Goodbye, Detective." She hung up before he had the chance to respond.

Hannah's head peeped over the cubicle wall. She didn't even look embarrassed. "So? Does the detective have a name?"

She'd told Hannah about the shooting in her apartment. There hadn't been much choice. Hannah's cousin lived on the first floor of the building. It was through Hannah that Claire and Nadine had found out about the available third-floor apartment.

"Vernelli. Sam Vernelli."

"Married?"

Hannah was thirty-eight and spent most of her evenings filling out profile sheets for online dating services. "No, I don't think so."

"Straight?"

Sam Vernelli radiated testosterone. "Pretty sure he is."

"Does he in any way resemble a troll?"

Claire smiled at her friend. "He's...very handsome." It was the truth and it begged the question of why he had never married. Was it possible that he was still in love with Tessa, that he'd never gotten over his first true love?

Or gotten over the guilt of harming her?

She was going to drive herself crazy. She deliberately looked at her watch. "Wow. Where is the day going? I better get busy." She grabbed the top file off the pile on her desk, opened it and pretended to read. When she heard the squeak of Hannah's chair, she started to breathe again. After another ten minutes, she quietly pulled her cell phone from her purse and left the office area. She took the elevator down to the lobby, exited the building and walked just far enough that she wasn't bothered by the smoke from the office workers who were huddled around the front door grabbing their morning nicotine fix.

She dialed Nadine's cell.

"Hey, Claire," Nadine answered.

"How's Omaha?"

"You know, nothing much changes in Omaha. What's going on there?"

"The police said that we can return to the apartment. I'll call the painter today."

"Thank goodness. So, do the police have any more thoughts on what might have happened?"

"Apparently not. When I did speak to Detective Vernelli this morning, he said that they were continuing to investigate."

There was a pause on the line. "What's to investigate?" Nadine finally asked. "She must have just been crazy."

"We could attest to that, right? I guess they intend to talk to the husband. I guess that's all probably routine."

"Yeah, sure. I thought you were going to ask for another detective to be assigned."

After the shooting, in between questions from the police, Claire had given Nadine the Cliff Notes version of her visit to Sam Vernelli's house the night before.

"I'm calling Detective Vernelli's boss next."

He'd come to her rescue—she was grateful for that. And he'd been decent about giving back her check. But none of that mattered. She detested Sam Vernelli.

Chapter Four

Sam sat in his car and watched Claire open the door to her apartment building. In deference to the unusually hot September, she wore white shorts, a red tank and flip-flops. She walked with purpose, her stride confident, the slight sway of her hips sexy. Her bare legs were tanned and firm with feminine muscle.

Suddenly feeling as if the necktie he still wore was choking him, he pulled it off and tossed it in the backseat. She'd really pushed his buttons this morning. She'd been just polite enough, just curt enough, just distant enough that he'd had no trouble visualizing himself as dirt on the bottom of the cute little white tennis shoes she'd worn that first day.

He wished he didn't care. Wished he didn't feel a sense of responsibility toward Tessa's sister. The Fontaines had hurt him badly when he'd most needed support. They'd put a target on his back and had done their best to ruin his life.

And Claire Fontaine had made it pretty clear—her loyalties lay with her parents.

But he had a case to solve. Yeah, it was still his case. Claire had made her call that morning. His boss had told him that. Had also told him that Claire had been pretty unhappy when he'd told her no. He said he might have considered it, but he was three detectives down and one more was hinting that he needed hernia surgery. His parting words to Sam had been, "Don't screw this up."

It was hard to screw up nothing. Which was about all he had. A woman with no apparent motive to harm Claire or Nadine had tried to kill them and now she was dead. None of it made any sense. That's what nagged at him. Not that he didn't believe in random acts of violence. He'd read through Tessa's murder investigation file often enough in those first years on the force that he couldn't dispute that sometimes horrible things just happened.

But more often than not, Sam believed that things happened for a reason. He just needed to figure out what those reasons were.

A white van pulled up and parked in front of Claire's building. Daybreak Professional Painters was scrawled across the side in red letters. When the driver opened the door, Sam judged him to be about forty. He had a belly and walked with a slight limp.

Harmless. See, nothing to worry about.

The driver slammed his car door and Sam saw big, beefy fingers, thick palms. Sam knew the damage that hands like that could do.

He reached for the door handle.

He stopped. What the hell was wrong with him? The guy was a referral from one of his own. He wasn't a homicidal maniac. Claire didn't need and certainly wouldn't appreciate his interference.

Sam watched the man walk into the apartment and managed to count to forty-five before thick, choking apprehension made his stomach turn and his legs move. He dodged across the street, cutting in front of an oncoming car. He ran up the three flights of stairs and knocked sharply.

The door swung open and Claire stared at him. He

looked over her head. Mr. Beefy-Hands was looking at the wall and scribbling notes on a yellow legal pad.

"I was in the neighborhood," he lied. "Thought I might stop by. My...uh...apartment could use some paint," he added. He was blabbering and he felt dangerously out of breath.

It could have been from taking the stairs two at a time but he thought it more likely was a result of being up close and personal with Claire's full breasts as they pushed against her thin knit shirt. The narrow straps on her shoulders were practically straining with the weight. Sam stepped into the apartment.

Claire didn't try to push him back out. She ignored him, acted as if he wasn't there and proceeded to negotiate Beefy-Hands down from what was a pretty good quote to begin with. Finally, with a nod in Sam's direction, the man left.

Claire walked over to the counter, picked up the man's card and handed it to Sam. "Here. Call him for your own quote."

He didn't bother to reach for the card. "I know I'm sticking my nose where it has no business being," he said. "But I'm concerned about you. Chicago is a big city and while 99.9 percent of the people are great, there's also scum out there."

"I don't want any favors from you, Detective Vernelli."

"Sam."

She shook her head. "We don't need to be on a first-name basis. I understand that this is going to be your case. I'm not happy about it, but quite frankly, I'm not going to spend a lot of time thinking about it. I expect you to do your job."

"You don't need to worry about that," he said, fighting back the urge to tell her just how good he was at his job.

He had a drawer full of commendations. But he had nothing to prove to her.

"If that's all, Detective, I need to get to my hotel before it gets dark."

"I'll drop you off."

She shook her head. The telephone rang, but she made no move to answer it. "Probably telemarketers," she said. "They're the only people who don't use our cell phones."

The answering machine kicked on. "Please leave a message."

"Pretty panties. Pretty Claire. Pretty Tessa." It was a man, his voice muffled. "Not that Tessa was so pretty when she was dead. Nasty two-by-four. Such a shame if the same thing happened to Claire."

Sam moved quickly but he still didn't reach the machine before they both heard the very final sounding click of the receiver.

"Son of a bitch," Sam said. He slammed his fist on the counter and his mouth was tight with fury. "Who the hell was that?"

Speechless, she shook her head.

"Think, Claire," Sam demanded. "Think."

She could hardly breathe, how could she think? My God, was it possible? It had been eleven years since Tessa had been killed. Who would say such a thing? What kind of cruel trick was this?

Sam pressed the rewind button on the answering machine and they listened to the horrible thing again. Then again. Until finally Claire put her hands over her ears. "Stop it, Sam. Stop it."

He chewed on his bottom lip. Then, very deliberately, he opened up the answering machine and lifted out the small tape. He dropped it in his pocket. His movements were jerky, almost mechanical in nature. His skin was pale and the dark pupils in the center of his brown eyes seemed bigger.

"I have to get this tape down to the station," he said. He looked her direction but sort of past her, as if there was something fascinating over her right shoulder.

"Tell me what you're thinking," she demanded.

"What do you know about Tessa's murder?" he asked, his voice low.

Only that it changed everything. "Not much," she admitted. "The details were always kept from me."

"That was probably best," he said, his voice even more subdued. "It wasn't pretty."

She must be in *The Twilight Zone.* No one in their right mind would have predicted that she'd be having this conversation with Sam Vernelli. Or that she'd have an insane urge to comfort him, to try to erase the grief that shadowed his eyes, narrowed his lips.

"What do you think happened, Sam?"

His head jerked up. "I thought you had a pretty good idea. Both you and your parents."

She wanted to defend herself, them, but she couldn't. Not when she was facing his absolute despair. "Tell me about it, Sam," she said gently.

He started pacing, making slow circles around her couch that someone from the police department had kindly covered with a sheet. "There were no witnesses and very little evidence at the scene," he said, his voice almost monotone. "Except what I left when I discovered her that morning. I touched her… I just couldn't believe that she could be dead.

"When the police came, I was a wreck. It's no wonder they didn't have trouble believing that I'd done it once your parents started pressuring them to look my direction."

"I heard you and Tessa arguing the day before."

He nodded. "I was worried that she wasn't going to pass

all her classes. She didn't take school seriously. Your sister was always the life of the party, everybody loved her. But she was drinking too much, too often. I told her she needed to stop. And if she didn't, she was going to be sorry. She wasn't listening and I got upset."

Claire wrapped her arms around her waist. "I've never heard anything about her drinking." However, Claire's parents had preached incessantly about the evils of teen drinking. Was it possible that he was telling the truth? Had her parents somehow been aware that Tessa had a problem and they'd been doubly focused on keeping Claire on the straight and narrow? There was no way of knowing. The only thing she knew for sure was that there was nothing to be gained now by arguing about it. "What did the police think happened?"

"They didn't have a clue. After I joined the force and read the investigation file, I realized how little evidence there was."

He said it without emotion, as if he'd come to terms with it.

"And what do you think now?"

"The same thing I thought when I saw your sister lying in a pool of blood on her kitchen floor with her head bashed in."

"What was that?"

"That, someday, I was going to get this guy, make him pay."

Claire swallowed hard. Her throat felt very dry. "You can't do that. You're a cop," she said.

He shrugged. "I loved her," he said simply.

Claire felt a pain deep inside, almost as if it radiated from her center. "I loved her, too. But it was eleven years ago," she said. "You need to let go."

"Let go? Let go?" he repeated, his voice louder.

"How do you even know it's a real threat? Maybe some crackpot heard about the recent shooting and somehow got my name. Then they searched online and information about Tessa's death came up."

He shook his head. "The newspapers said that she'd been beaten. They never said anything about the two-by-four. I knew it because I found her. The only other place I've ever seen the details was in the police report."

"But—"

"I've got to get this to the lab, blow up the background noise, hopefully get a lead," he said. He opened the front door just inches, then shut it. He turned to look at her. "You should go back to Nebraska."

It was the very last thing she intended to do. Her parents would demand an explanation. She'd be lucky if they didn't arrange a twenty-four-hour guard. "No," she said, wanting to keep it simple.

He studied her. "Your parents don't know about any of this, do they? About Sandy Bird, the robbery?"

He had good intuition. It was probably what made him a good detective. "What I tell my parents isn't really any of your business."

"Why?"

"Because I didn't even know you until—"

He waved a hand impatiently. "I know why you want me keeping my nose out of it. What I don't understand is why you won't tell your parents."

She sighed. "Since I was thirteen, my parents have pretty much lived in a constant state of worry, just terrified that something was going to happen to me. I hurt them when I insisted upon coming to Chicago like Tessa. I won't hurt them more by sharing the grim details of what has happened in the last week. I'm not sure they could survive it."

"I'm sorry," he said. He leaned his head against the door and closed his eyes. Finally he opened them. "I guess I never really thought about what it must have been like for you."

She didn't want his sympathy. But it suddenly didn't seem right to fling it back in his face. "I think we can agree that I didn't walk a mile in your moccasins either."

He rubbed a hand across his jaw. "Look, it's not safe for you to stay here."

"I'll go back to the hotel. I was planning on staying there until this place got repainted anyway."

Sam shook his head. "Maybe this guy is watching you. Maybe he knows where you're staying."

It made her skin crawl. "Fine. I'll stay somewhere else." Where, she had no idea. Hannah would certainly offer up a couch, but there was no way she wanted to involve anybody else in this mess.

He stared at her. "You could stay at my house."

It was so unexpected that she leaned against the kitchen counter for support. "What?"

"Just for a few days. Just until I can get my head around this, figure out the next steps."

She couldn't figure out anything. It was all a confusing mess. Tessa had loved this man, had planned to marry him. Yet, her parents believed he'd had something to do with her death. "I...I can't."

He ran his hand through his short hair. "You're afraid of me, aren't you? Afraid to be in my house because maybe I am some whack job who took a two-by-four to your sister?" His voice was laced with pain.

"It's too complicated," she said. Before she could add any other explanation, he pulled his cell phone out of his pocket.

"I'm going to simplify it." He motioned her close and

tilted the phone away from his ear, allowing her to hear the person on the other end. She listened as he succinctly told his boss about the threat and that he intended to stash her at his house.

He ended the call and slammed his cell phone shut. "Do I need to take an ad out in the paper, too? Perhaps a photo of me with a caption that says lock this man up if something happens to Claire Fontaine?"

He was obnoxious and insulting and she wanted to fire back, but she didn't. She'd hurt him. Badly. "Don't push it, Sam," she said, wanting him to know that she understood, but that she still wasn't going to be bullied. "I'll need a few minutes to get some clothes packed."

THEY DIDN'T TALK on the fifteen-minute drive to his house, and Sam was okay with that. He didn't want to argue about her staying, didn't want to talk about Tessa and he sure as hell didn't want to talk about the tape that was burning a hole in his pocket. Instead, he watched the traffic around him, took a few unnecessary turns and was confident that nobody had followed him.

He parked on the street and they walked up the steps. As he unlocked the front door, he turned. "I hope you're not allergic to dogs," he said.

"I don't think so. I never had one."

"Yeah, well, just watch your shoes. He likes to chew."

Once inside, Nightmare came running. When he saw Claire, he did a little circle thing with his body, wagged his tail so hard that it hit the wall, and acted like he'd fallen paws first into love. It didn't help that Claire dropped her bag, sunk to her knees and wrapped her arms around the big, black moose.

"Oh, you're so pretty."

Nightmare put his nose in the air, like he understood

that he'd finally arrived. Somebody appreciated him. "Great watchdog," Sam said. "Maybe you could show her where the silverware is." He looked at Claire. "Not that I have any good silverware or that I think you'd be interested in it if I did."

Claire smiled.

And she sparkled. Even with tired eyes, she lit up the room and he felt the same shortness of breath that had hit him when she'd opened her apartment door earlier. Maybe he had some kind of lung disease.

Nightmare rolled over and let Claire pat his stomach. "Oh, you sweet thing," Claire crooned.

Sam could swear the dog had a grin on his face.

Sam led her into the kitchen, where he stuck his head in the fridge. "There's some soda and some beer. I'm sorry, I don't have any wine." He straightened up and shut the door. With a long stretch, he grabbed the newspapers off the table and dumped them into the wastebasket at the end of his counter. He picked up the open box of cereal next to his stove and shoved it into a cupboard. Looking over his shoulder, he said, "I would have cleaned."

Claire shrugged. "Looks lived-in. I hate houses where everything has to be just so. It's like you can't even breathe in them."

Sam turned his head away from her and stared inside the cupboard at the boxes of cereal, the peanut butter and the cookies that he hadn't been able to resist. If Sam remembered right, Lucille Fontaine, of the Fontaine Fixture dynasty, had been a neat-freak. She'd kept a live-in maid busy full-time just dusting and sweeping their twenty-room mansion. For months after Tessa's murder, when the police were still circling, he'd dreamed of those bedrooms. Dreamed about being locked up and when his parents had come to find him, the Fontaines had moved him to another bedroom, then another. Until finally his family had given up and gone away.

He slammed the open cupboard door shut. "I'm out of here," he said. "I'll be late, so…just go to bed whenever you want. Second door on the right is the extra bedroom. I've got a computer in there and some weights, but if you can walk around that, the futon is pretty comfortable. Bathroom is at the end of the hall."

She waved a hand. "It'll be fine."

She was wrong. Nothing had really been fine for a long time. "Please don't leave the house. It's possible you might hear someone on the back stairs. I rent the third floor to Dolores Ames and her son, Tom. Their number is right here." He pointed to a margarita-glass magnet on the refrigerator.

"If anything seems odd," he continued on, "call 9-1-1. Don't hesitate. Just do it."

"I will. I'll be fine. We don't even know that I'm in any danger. The caller might just have been trying to shake me up."

Yeah, well, he'd shaken things up. Sam felt as if his insides were in a blender. "Just be alert," he said as he pulled the door shut behind him. As he hurried down the steps, he was pushing buttons on his cell phone. When Cruz answered, Sam didn't waste time. "I need you to meet me at the station. I've got a tape of a call that Claire got on her answering machine."

"Who has answering machines with tapes anymore?"

"We're lucky that Claire and Nadine did." It was an old one, probably something the Fontaines had in their basement and insisted Claire take with her. They wouldn't want their calls missed.

"Who left the message?" Cruz asked.

"I don't know." All he really knew was that he was a

thread away from being completely unraveled. "Maybe from the robber? He knew about the panties. The guy also knew about Tessa. He said that Claire and Tessa were pretty, but that Tessa…that Tessa hadn't been so pretty when she was dead and wouldn't it be too bad if the same thing happened to Claire."

He heard Cruz suck in a breath, but his partner didn't say anything.

"Well?" Sam prompted, fighting the urge to slam his fist through his car window.

"Are you okay, Sam?" Cruz asked.

He was so far from okay that he could even remember what it looked like. "I need your help, Cruz. We have got to find this guy."

"How's Claire?"

Shocked. Scared, maybe. In denial, for sure. He hadn't taken the time to really analyze it. He couldn't stay. Every time he'd looked at her, he'd seen a young blond-haired girl, her head bashed in, her light extinguished. "She's okay," he said. "I've got her stashed at my house."

"If you want to stay with her, I'll take the tape in."

"No." Eleven years ago he hadn't been able to finish it. This time he would. Whatever it took, he'd do it.

Chapter Five

Twenty minutes later, Sam pulled the investigation file on Tessa's murder. It was yellowed with age and smelled like a file smells when it's been boxed away. When it's been forgotten.

Never.

He owed Tessa more than that.

"You really think the person who called Claire had something to do with the robbery and Tessa's murder?" Cruz asked. "And what does that have to do with Sandy Bird?"

"I don't know." Sam opened the flap and pulled out the contents. Loose pictures of Tessa, facedown on the tile floor where she'd fallen, slipped out.

Cruz reached over, picked one up, studied it, then put it back, facedown. "If that was Meg…" he said, his voice trailing off. "You know, Sam, no one would think less of you if you went home and let me review the file."

"I can't do that."

Cruz shrugged. "I didn't think so." He held out his hand. "Give me half of that."

A half hour later, Sam felt like he'd been sucked back eleven years, that it was the beginning of the summer between his junior and senior year in college, and he had the world by the tail. He had a calling—journalism. He had a great love—Tessa. He'd had it all.

Then, in the blink of an eye, the time it takes to crush a person's skull, he had nothing.

He'd first seen Tessa Fontaine three weeks into his freshman year. They'd been at a dorm party, the kind where noise and guests and beer spill out into the hallway and the lobby. In the corner of said lobby, Tessa's date for the night had seemed determined to stick his tongue down Tessa's throat every chance he got.

Not that Tessa had seemed to mind all that much.

And that should have been enough for Sam to turn the other way, to start looking for his own entertainment—in those days, it would have been the closest game of poker. But there'd been something about the long-legged, blond-haired beauty that had drawn and kept his attention.

That had ended up being a very good thing for Tessa. When her date had led her to an empty room at the end of the hallway, Sam had been close enough to hear the first scream. He'd gotten inside the room, landed his fist solidly into the guy's nose, and hustled Tessa out of the room before anybody else noticed the young woman with the front of her shirt ripped from collar to waist.

They'd spent the night in his dorm room. Talking. Him in the desk chair and Tessa sitting on the bed, dwarfed by one of his T-shirts. He'd fallen first in lust and then in love, but they'd come so quick on the heels of one another that he'd been hard-pressed at eighteen to separate the difference.

By Christmas, they'd been sleeping together. When they'd parted at break, and she'd gone home to her big house in Nebraska and he'd gone back to Minnesota, he'd wondered how he might survive.

He'd told Jake about her and his brother, home on leave

from the service, had given him a case of condoms for Christmas. He'd understood the subtle message. Nobody needed to tell him not to screw up his plans, his dreams. How would he be a great journalist and earn a Pulitzer before he was thirty if he didn't finish college?

When he'd returned to school for the spring semester and she'd fallen into his arms, all had been right with the world. They'd been inseparable for sophomore and junior year and senior year, on her twenty-second birthday, he'd asked her to marry him. Three weeks later, she was dead.

It had been relatively quick, or so the medical examiner had said. That statement, no doubt meant to bring comfort, had brought none. He'd gone through the motions of life, attending her funeral, helping her roommates pack up her things, throwing away the toiletries she'd kept at his apartment.

And then there'd been the circus of accusations and questions and even threats. *Just tell us the truth.* That's what the police had said to him.

The truth was the downward spiral that had started when he gathered Tessa's cold body in his arms was gaining speed.

After the police had officially discounted him as a suspect, he'd quietly fallen apart. He'd stopped going to school, stopped eating, living mostly on alcohol and sleeping pills.

When he'd gone home for Thanksgiving his senior year, he'd seen the despair in his parents' eyes. But it hadn't mattered. He'd gone back to Chicago but didn't attend a single class between Thanksgiving and Christmas.

He failed every one of his classes that term and when it came time to sign up for classes for the spring semester, he didn't bother. He barely bothered to get out of bed.

Nothing mattered. Tessa was dead.

His parents had insisted he come home. His mother had coddled, his father had bullied, and he'd started fantasizing about ways to kill himself. He blew off the appointments with the psychologist, refused to talk to the priest that his mother dragged home and spent most of the days sleeping.

He was a train wreck.

His parents, worn down by the strain of the looming possibility that they were losing their son, fought constantly. The weekend that Sam should have graduated from college, his father moved out. Sam hadn't even come out of the basement to say goodbye.

If Jake hadn't come home when he did from his thank-you-very-much-Uncle-Sam tour of duty, taken one look at him and literally dragged him up the basement stairs, he knew he'd be dead by now.

He'd dried out and in the process had realized he wasn't dried up. He'd returned to school in the fall, changed his major to law enforcement and graduated three semesters later. His parents had found their way back, too, to each other, to him.

And he'd managed to get on with his life. Had forgotten about getting a Pulitzer and had focused on getting scum off the street. And told himself that if he wasn't happy, he was at least content.

It had been enough.

And then, damn it, Claire Fontaine had waltzed into his life.

Beautiful. Sexy. Smart.

Vulnerable.

He looked back down at the file. He'd read every word many times. And he was going to do it all again. He couldn't afford to miss anything.

Claire couldn't afford for him to miss anything.

Three hours later, he looked up to see Cruz smother a

yawn. Sam reached over and snagged the half of the file that Cruz had been reading. He stuffed it into his backpack. "Go home," he said.

"We could probably both use some sleep," Cruz said, pushing his chair back from his desk.

Sam didn't want to close his eyes ever again. But he nodded and the two men walked out to the mostly deserted parking lot. He drove home. When he got there, he sat in his dark car, staring up at his dark windows.

He was so weary. Not just from tonight. From everything. From years of pretending that he didn't mind coming home to a dark, empty house. From the stress of being slap-happy for his brother Jake who was going to be a father any day, but knowing deep down that it wasn't ever going to happen for him. From being afraid, truly afraid, to ever love again.

Whoever had said that it was better to have loved and lost had never really lost. It was better just to make do, to keep on pretending that this was the life you picked, wanted even.

Sam let himself into the quiet house. The first thing he noticed was that Nightmare didn't come to greet him. The second, that Claire had washed the few dirty dishes that had been in the sink. Quietly, he walked down the hallway. He didn't want to stop, didn't want to check on her, but he couldn't make himself go past.

He pushed open the door and froze. She was wearing a nightgown. It was white, cotton, and probably respectable when she stood up. But right now, she was lying on her side and it had ridden up practically to her waist. He could see the feminine curve of her upper leg, the bright blue silk of her underwear.

And like some goofball, he heard the old playground chant: *I see London, I see France. I see Claire's under-*

pants. Nightmare, who lay at the end of the bed, cocked his head as if he couldn't wait to see where this was going. Sam, feeling a little light-headed, backed out of the room.

Nowhere. It was going nowhere.

SAM CHECKED ON CLAIRE three times during the night and was careful to keep his eyes focused shoulder-height and above. It would have been nice if she'd snored and drooled, but she slept like a lady, her mouth shut and her breathing even.

At six, when he poked his head in the door, she had her eyes open, and he felt about as edgy as he'd felt the night before when he'd tucked his tail between his legs and run. "Good morning," he said. "How do you feel?"

"Rested," she admitted. "You were right, it's a pretty comfortable futon." She smiled at Nightmare, who lay on top of the blanket, across her lower legs.

"Get off," he said. "You're a nuisance."

She reached out and patted the dog. "You're fine. Don't listen to him."

Sam sighed. "Not to worry. It hasn't been a problem in the past."

She laughed and then, as if she suddenly remembered where she was, she stopped. "I sort of crashed last night," she said. "I didn't even hear you come home."

"You'd had a big day," he said.

She chewed on the corner of her pretty lip. "Any thoughts about who might have made the call?"

He shook his head. "Not yet, but we'll figure it out."

She nodded. He wasn't sure she was convinced or if she just didn't have the energy to argue about it. Maybe the time, he decided, when she swung her tanned legs over the side of the bed.

"I guess I better get dressed for work," she said. "Is that coffee?" she asked hopefully, sniffing the air.

"Yes," he said. "I can get you some," he said, grateful for the excuse to move, to do something.

"I'll get it," she said. "Please don't wait on me. Just pretend I'm not here."

Hard to do when she'd changed the look, the feel and especially the smell of his house. The spare room had a spicy, woman scent. Hell, even Nightmare seemed to smell better.

"If you like pancakes, I made some batter," he said.

"I didn't expect that," she said, looking unsure.

"I have to eat anyway," he said. "There are towels on the counter in the bathroom."

"Thank you," she said. She stared somewhere above his head. "I appreciate this. All of it."

"No problem," he said.

He walked back to the kitchen, flipped on CNN, turned it up loud and pretended that he had nothing better to do than concentrate on the latest mayhem in the Middle East. He was definitely not thinking about her standing naked in his shower. No way, nohow.

Twenty-two minutes later, when she walked into the kitchen, all clean and shiny, smelling incredibly good, wearing a black dress, he told himself that he had it all under control.

Then she reached to pull a coffee cup off his shelf and her dress went with her.

He burned the palm of his hand on the griddle and when he jerked back, he knocked the syrup bottle off the counter. The heavy plastic hit the floor with a thud.

"Can I help?" she asked, looking over her shoulder.

"You're short," he accused.

Her cheeks got pink. "I know. Being five-three is a

curse. I can't reach anything. I spend a lot of time crawling on and off step stools."

If she did that, her breasts might be right around eye-
level. "That's dangerous," he said.

She shrugged. "Is there a bus stop close by? I usually
walk to work but your apartment is about ten blocks farther."

"I can drop you off. It's no trouble."

She shook her head. "Absolutely not. If there's no bus,
I'll walk it."

One by one, he flipped all six of the pancakes. She
was short *and* stubborn. "Fine. There's a stop two blocks
north, at the corner." He opened the oven door and pulled
out the plates he'd put inside to warm. He slid three pancakes onto her plate.

She took a deep breath. "They smell good. I don't cook
very much," she admitted. "Just pasta." She took her time
spreading butter on the pancakes and then added syrup.
Then she carefully cut a bite and chewed.

"Perfect," she said, her eyes lighting up.

Yeah, she was.

And she was Tessa's sister.

He sat down, facing the television, making sure she realized he didn't intend to talk his way through breakfast.
It didn't seem to bother her. She ate little bites, delicately
sipped her coffee and read the newspaper.

Not that he was watching or anything.

He shoved his chair back and took his empty plate over
to the sink. "I've got to get going. Here's an extra key.
Make sure you lock the bolt lock."

She nodded. "I guess I'll see you tonight."

That probably wasn't a good idea. "I might be working.
It could be very late. You'll probably be sleeping."

"Man. I thought *I* was a Type A."

WHEN SAM OPENED HIS DOOR that evening, he heard Jimmy Buffet, he smelled spaghetti sauce and he saw Claire Fontaine's shoes underneath his kitchen table. Nightmare, lying on a rug in front of the refrigerator, raised his head.

"You are such a traitor," Sam said. "There's good leather there and you're ignoring it."

Nightmare rested his head on his paws. Sam walked to the stove, picked up a spoon and stirred the bubbling sauce. He sniffed and thought he might be in heaven. He hadn't had time for lunch and he'd figured dinner would be cereal.

He certainly hadn't expected her to cook for him. He turned down the flame under the sauce, then stooped to scratch Nightmare's head. Then he heard a thud from his spare room and what might have been a groan.

He pulled his gun. When he rounded the corner, he stopped. Claire lay on his exercise bench, her back flat, her legs spread, one on each side of the gray vinyl-covered bench. Her eyes were closed, her lips pressed together in concentration, and her arms were extended, with a twenty-pound weight in each hand. With short, panting-like breaths, she began her reps, lifting the weights up over her body, letting them meet in the middle, holding, then releasing.

Her short hair, damp around the edges, curled around her neck and her delicate collarbone glistened with perspiration. And with each lift, her breasts, covered by a tight, white exercise top with thin straps, squeezed together.

Up. Down. Up. Down. Sleek arm muscle rippled, polished skin gleamed and the pulse in the hollow of her neck throbbed.

At a cadence matching his own growing need.

Where the top stopped, the shorts didn't start. At least three inches of tanned, smooth skin showed. With each lift, her slick stomach contracted, the muscles creating a line of clear definition right down the center. He followed it until it disappeared into her shorts.

Oh, damn, her shorts. Thin, clingy, starting an inch below her navel and ending miles above her knees.

He could see the points of her hip bones, the gentle rounding of her abdomen and lower still, the sharp rise of her pubic bone.

Oh, baby.

He might have actually said it because she dropped the weights with a thud and sat up. "Hi," she said, a little out of breath. "You scared me."

She still had her legs spread. He could not think, let alone speak.

"Sam?"

"Yes."

"Why do have your gun?"

He stared at it. He was never, ever, careless with his gun and he'd forgotten it was in his hand. He slid it back in his shoulder holster. "I heard a noise."

She slid her bottom along the bench and for one second, Sam imagined her sliding her warm, sweaty body against his. He could almost feel her moist heat, her female warmth. His body tightened in response.

When she got to the end, she put her legs together and stood. It took everything he had not to push her back down, spread her legs again and grind himself against her, muscle to muscle, need to need.

"I made dinner," she said, wiping her face with a hand towel. "Pasta, of course." She looked uncomfortable. "Payback for breakfast, you know."

He was hungry. That was it. That explained why his legs felt like spaghetti and his head seemed empty. Her scent, the spice he sniffed this morning now mixed with feminine energy, danced around him. Desire, sharp and angry, twisted and sick, clawed at him.

He wanted her. He wanted her in his bed. It took his breath away. What kind of bastard was he? He'd offered her protection, a safe place to stay and now he wanted to rip her clothes off and bury himself inside her warm and yielding body.

"I hope you don't mind that I used your equipment."

His *equipment* wouldn't mind at all.

Yep, no doubt about it. He was a sick, sick man. "No, that's fine."

She placed one leg in front of the other and lunged, stretching her muscles.

He wanted her legs, all firm and toned, wrapped around his waist.

She cocked her head. "Are you okay?"

No. Just confused. She was the one who'd been lifting weights, but he was the one who was all hot and bothered. "I'm fine," he said, waving away her concern.

She walked past him.

Oh, baby, was there anything sexier than the delicate muscles in a woman's back?

She turned. "I think I'll take a quick shower. Would you mind if I watch something on television tonight?"

"A chick flick?" he asked.

"The Cubs are in San Diego. It's a late game."

"You like baseball?"

Her face lit up and her eyes danced. "You're looking at the starting pitcher for the Minooka Timberwolves. I don't get to talk about it much. Nadine hates sports—turns off the television or radio even when they're giving the sports news. But I love professional baseball, especially in the fall, when every game counts so much."

Could this get much worse? He had to put a stop to it now. "Look, I can't stay for dinner."

"Oh."

She had the biggest, prettiest eyes.

"That's okay," she said. "I just took a chance. It'll reheat. You can have spaghetti for lunch tomorrow."

He'd never look at spaghetti again without thinking of her. "So, how old are you?"

"Twenty-four," she said, sounding puzzled at the sudden shift in topic.

That's what he thought. "Are you involved with anybody right now?"

"What?"

"Are you dating anybody?"

She shook her head.

Damn. "You should date," he instructed. "Girls your age should have boyfriends. Go to parties. Dancing. Fun stuff."

She stared at him like he'd lost his mind. He was pretty sure he had. It had burst into flames when it had fallen below his belt. "Now's not the time for you," he said, "to get serious with anyone. Definitely not."

Now she looked really confused. "I just told you, I'm not serious about anyone. Why are we having this conversation?"

No way was he going there. "You should have a waiting list," he said, spreading his arms wide. "Guys on the front burners and on the back, too. That's what girls your age do. They date, they shop around. They experiment."

Her big brown eyes opened even wider. "You think I need to experiment?"

She was killing him. "Yeah, I do."

She rubbed her forehead. "I'll try to remember that," she said, sounding weary.

Chapter Six

Three beers later, Sam felt marginally better. He shifted on his worn plastic barstool and caught Patrick Murphy's eye.

"Hey, Sammy, my boy." The brawny man sauntered over. He wore a white shirt and dark pants, covered with a big red apron. He ruffled up the back of Sam's hair. "I don't see you in here that often anymore. How's that pretty mother of yours?"

"Still married to my father," Sam said, shaking his head. It had been three years since he'd brought his parents to Murphy's for a drink and Patrick Murphy, who had passed sixty sometime back, had taken one look at Sam's mother and fallen head over Irish heels in love.

"He's a lucky man. Two sons and a beautiful wife. How much good fortune can a man have?" Patrick inclined his head toward Sam's empty glass, but Sam shook his head no. More beer wasn't going to make a difference.

"What about you, Sam? When are you going to find a pretty girl and marry her? Have fine sons and daughters of your own?"

A week ago he'd have laughed off the question. Said something about balls and chains and cheap construction in the suburbs. But now, the question settled over him like an ominous, dark cloud. Maybe it was the impending status of uncle. Maybe it was his mother and her eight months of nonstop chatter about grandchildren. Maybe it was Cruz, a man lost because his marriage had gone bust for seemingly no reason at all.

Maybe it was the memories of Tessa and the young girl he'd almost married. Maybe it was knowing that if Tessa had lived, everything would have been different.

It sure as hell wasn't that he liked coming home to Claire.

If he wanted spaghetti, Patrick's cook could whip up a mean sauce. If he wanted big brown eyes and a warm body, he could snuggle up to Nightmare. If he wanted breasts, he could buy a magazine or rent a movie.

"Well?" Patrick prodded.

"I'm too old and set in my ways," he said. "What woman would have me?"

"I was older than you when I married my Colleen. She was a beauty. Still was when she died twenty-four years later."

Sam could see the misery in the man's watery blue eyes. "I'm sorry I never got to meet your wife. She must have been special."

"Aye. Cancer is a cruel beast. But I'm glad that I had her company for so many years. She could have done better, but she chose me."

"Where did you meet her?" Sam asked, knowing the man wanted to talk, wanted to remember.

"I met her at her parents' home. Her pa had hired me to help put a roof on the house, never dreaming that I'd steal his daughter away. Almost killed me when he found out that she'd been sneaking out at night. After all, her being only seventeen and all."

"Seventeen? How old were you?"

"Old enough to know that I'd found something special. I was thirty-three. A man."

Sixteen years. Wow. "You're lucky her father didn't push you off the roof when you weren't looking."

"Believe me, long after the garage had a new roof, I stayed far away when he had a hammer in his hand."

"What changed?"

Patrick sat down on the stool next to Sam. He turned it so that he was facing out at the crowd, and then leaned back against the wood bar, as if he was royalty watching over his kingdom. "I think he realized that I loved her dearly and that it was mutual. I think he saw, too, that age is a number. When a boy is sixteen and a girl is a baby, the difference is forever. Even when a man is twenty-eight and the girl is barely gracing twelve, it's a river too wide and deep to cross. But when a man is thirty-nine and his bride is twenty-three, the river dwindles to a small stream. When the man is forty-five and the twenty-nine-year-old woman bears him a child, the sixteen years are a blessing."

Sixteen? Nine? None of that mattered. He'd just gotten surprised tonight. Hadn't expected to find a sweaty, half-naked woman in his spare room. Hadn't expected that he'd react like a teenager. Hadn't expected that she'd look so hurt when he'd pushed her away.

"I've got to go," he said, getting to his feet. "I'll see you later."

"Don't be a stranger," Murphy called after him.

He wasn't a stranger, but he was acting pretty damn strange. He needed to get a grip. He would not be undone by a pair of brown eyes. He would not grovel, beg or via any similar action or reaction, let it be known that he'd taken one look at her legs and almost sworn off breasts. Almost.

There was no sense going overboard.

Sam walked at a slow pace and let the air clear his head. He felt almost normal by the time he got home. That is, until he discovered that his house was empty. Claire's cell phone and purse were lying on the table next to the futon.

He found the note on his second pass through the kitchen. *I took Nightmare for a run.*

In the dark? What was she thinking? He looked at his watch. The ten o'clock news had just started.

Did she have any idea of what could happen to a woman at night? Did she really think some stupid dog could protect her? One little bullet, right between the eyes, and Nightmare would be down for the count.

Where would she go? There was a park about three blocks away. Would she head that direction? Did she even know about it? Would she just walk the streets?

He grabbed his keys and was halfway out the door before he stopped. He'd had three beers on an empty stomach. Not enough that he felt anything, but maybe just enough to put him over the legal limit.

Jamie Donaldson's face flashed before his eyes. Jamie had been one of the best detectives on the force. One night, coming home from a party, well over the legal limit, he'd hit two twelve-year-olds as they crossed the street. The girls had been dead before the paramedics arrived. Not only had Jamie about lost his mind, he'd lost his job and more. He was doing five to ten at Joliet, sharing cell space with scum that he'd helped put away.

No way would he get behind the wheel of a car. If he got caught, it could cost him everything.

Yeah, but, not doing anything could cost Claire her life.

He pounded on his tenant's door and waited impatiently. He knocked again and finally Tom Ames opened the door. He wore ratty black shorts, a T-shirt with a huge hole under one arm and reading glasses perched on the end of his nose. White acne medication dotted his face. He held an open, four-inch-thick microbiology textbook up to his chest. "Sam?" he asked.

"I'm sorry to bother you," Sam said. "But I need your help."

"*You* need *my* help?"

"Yeah. I need to go look for a friend who took Nightmare for a walk. I can't drive. I had a couple beers earlier tonight."

Tom, who was working on his second master's degree, nodded. Tom's mother worked for the department and no doubt Tom, too, had heard the story of Jamie Donaldson. "Let me get my keys," he said.

"Is your mom home?"

"No. She's working nights for the next month."

Two minutes later, Tom eased his car away from the curb. He drove with both hands on the wheel while Sam sat on the passenger side, his nose practically pressed up to the window. "Circle the block," Sam said.

"Okay. Who exactly is it that we're looking for?"

"Her name is Claire. She's short, dark-haired, about your age. She might be wearing a white shirt and yellow shorts." *Please, please, let her at least have had the good sense to change clothes. Something that covered all her parts.* Sam resisted the urge to cross himself, to make it an official prayer.

The streetlights made it easy enough to see the sidewalk. It was a warm fall night and couples, both young and old, strolled along, hand in hand. They didn't worry him. The group of kids hanging on the front step of one of the brownstones warranted a second look.

"Slow down," he said. There wasn't anything much more dangerous to a lone woman than a group of testosterone-charged teenage boys. It happened once or twice a year. One idiot would get an idea and then normally good boys,

boys with futures and plans, would follow, forever altering their lives and the life of the victim.

"Want to get out?" Tom asked.

"No, keep driving," Sam said. It looked like this group of boys was focused on their card game.

They circled the block twice, giving Sam a chance to inspect both sides of the street. No Claire. Not anywhere.

"Head down toward Patriot's Park," he said. When Tom pulled up outside the wrought-iron gate that marked the park's entrance, Sam jumped from the car. "Stay here," he said. "I'm going to check the running path."

"You don't look like you're dressed for a run."

Sam looked down at his now-wrinkled suit and dress shoes. He'd been home twice since he'd dressed this morning. Both times he'd rushed out. Once to avoid Claire, and now, to find her. He could take his jacket off, but then his shoulder holster would be in full view. He wanted the benefit of surprise if Claire was in trouble.

Fifteen minutes later Sam had run every path. He'd pounded down the cinder-covered trail, sweating like a dog, no doubt scaring the hell out of people going for a late-night stroll.

When he got back to Tom's car, he leaned against it, breathing heavy. He dialed her cell phone number, listening impatiently while the phone rang. When it switched over to voice mail, he slammed his phone shut and jerked open the door. "Let's go. Head back toward my house, but take Trainer Street this time." It was the high-rent district, but that didn't mean it was any safer.

He saw Nightmare before he saw Claire. The dog lay on the sidewalk, his head on his paws, in front of a three-story brownstone. Claire, dressed in long pants and a loose T-shirt, *thank You, Lord,* sat three steps up next to a man. She didn't look hurt, harmed or scared.

That didn't help the ball of angry fire heating up in Sam's belly. "Stop the car," he ordered.

Tom pressed the brakes and the car skidded to a stop. "There's no place to park," he said.

"We won't be staying long," Sam said, opening his door. He reached Claire in nine strides. He counted them, trying to get his emotions under control. It didn't work.

"What the hell are you doing?" he asked.

"Sam?" Claire's head jerked up in surprise.

"What are you thinking? You must be some kind of fool."

The guy next to Claire shifted, like he wasn't sure if he should run or not dare make a move. Sam pointed his finger at the man. "Sit. This is none of your business. And who the hell are you anyway?"

The man opened his mouth, but no words came out.

Claire frowned at Sam. "Sam, this is Pete Mission. We work together. Pete, this is Sam, the detective I was telling you about."

When Claire smiled at the guy, the heat in Sam's gut turned up a notch. "Kind of late for a business meeting, isn't it?"

She frowned at him. "Pete and I are both finalists in a design contest. There's an awards dinner early next week. We were making a few plans."

"Whatever," Sam said. "Can we just get out of here?"

She got up and dusted off her butt. Sam didn't miss that Pete's eyes followed the motion. He might have to kill the guy after all.

Claire walked down the steps, her pretty pointed chin in the air. "You look a little flustered, Sam," she said.

Flustered? Sam Vernelli didn't do flustered. "I couldn't find you," he said.

"I left a note," she said, bending down to grab Night-mare's leash.

A car pulled up behind Tom's car and the driver leaned on his horn. Sam grabbed Claire's elbow and steered her toward the car. "We'll talk about this later," he said. "Just do what I say."

She stopped, dead in the middle of the street. The man in the car stuck his head out of the window and started yelling in Spanish. Dogs up and down the street started barking. Lights flipped on. Window shades went up.

It was a damn circus.

Sam yanked on her arm and barely budged her. For a little thing, she'd dug her heels in. Literally.

"Come on," he said. "You're making a scene."

She turned on him. "*I'm* making a scene? How dare you?"

"I swear to God, Claire, if you don't move, I'm going to throw you over my shoulder and carry you to that car."

"You wouldn't dare."

The guy, still screaming, opened his car door.

Sam leaned down, put his shoulder next to her stomach and upended her.

She shrieked. Then kicked.

And for one crazy minute, he let himself fantasize about spanking her feisty butt.

He held her legs down with one hand and yanked open the car door with the other. Nightmare, for once acting like he had a brain, jumped in without prodding. Sam dumped Claire onto the seat and slid in after her.

"Drive," he said.

Tom, scrubbing at his acne medicine with one hand, reached his other arm over the seat. "Hi. I'm Tom. I live above Sam."

Claire, acting like she was at some damn tea party, extended her own hand. "It's a pleasure to meet you."

"Could we hold off on the introductions for a few minutes?" Sam asked, furious with both of them. Horn Blower had gone back to his car, but Sam figured, given his luck lately, it was only to retrieve a gun from under the seat.

"Of course," Tom said, winking at Claire.

Claire winked back.

What was there to wink about? If Tom had started beating his head against the window and pulling out his hair, now *that* would have made some sense.

When they got to Sam's house, it took Tom two tries to squeeze back into his parking spot. Sam barely waited for the car to stop moving before he opened the door and got out. Then he tapped his fingers against the hood of the car. Nightmare came out first, followed closely by Claire. She moved quickly. He had to slam the car door and chase her up the front steps of his house. He could hear Tom running behind him.

Claire had shoved a key into the lock by the time he caught her. He heard the tumblers fall into place and he reached past her to shove the door open. Nightmare darted in.

But suddenly Claire didn't move. She turned to look at him. "I'm sorry. I acted like a fool at Pete's place. I get a little crazy when people tell me what to do."

"It's because we're Generation Y," Tom said from somewhere behind him.

Tom made it sound like Sam was Generation Old.

"Can we please just call it a night?" Sam asked.

Claire nodded.

"Hope to see you again, Claire," Tom called out.

"Sure. That would be great," Claire said, finally stepping inside.

Yeah. Great. Sam shut the door harder than he needed to.

"Nice guy," Claire said.

"If you like the nose-in-the-book type," Sam said. He did not want to talk about Tom. "It's late," he said.

"Why was he driving you?"

"I'd had a couple of beers. Didn't want to take a chance."

"Oh." She walked into the kitchen and got herself a glass of water. She stood at the sink, drinking it. "You know it's been just recently," she said, "that I've started to say no. That I wasn't going to do exactly what I was told." She gave him a small smile. "Trust me on this one, that's a good thing, but I went a little overboard tonight. I caused you a problem and I shouldn't have. I really am sorry."

Could she make him feel any more miserable? "Forget it," Sam said. "You're okay and that's all that matters."

She nodded. "Did you get any dinner?"

"Don't worry about me," he said. His stomach was still in knots. He wouldn't be eating anytime soon.

She chewed on one fingernail. "Well, then, I guess I'll go to bed." She walked down the hallway and Nightmare fell in step next to her. She had her hand on the doorknob to the spare room when his cell phone rang.

Sam snagged it. "Hello," he said.

"Sam, honey."

"My mother," he whispered and when Claire smiled, his knees felt a little weak. He leaned back against the kitchen counter, grateful for the support. It was crazy, but he really didn't want her to be mad at him.

"Sam, we have the best news."

His mother was practically screaming. Sam held the phone a couple inches away from his ear. "I bet you're a grandma."

"Yes. At four this morning." His mother's voice returned to almost normal. "And she's perfect. Ten toes, ten fingers. We went to the hospital to see her tonight. She has the most wonderful strawberry-blond hair."

A baby girl. Damn. Jake had a daughter. "How's Joanna?"

"Fine, but tired. She was in labor most of the night."

"And Jake?"

"He's a wreck. Your father was the same way. I swear, big, tough men are the worst. Can't handle childbirth. It's a good thing the Vernelli men marry strong women. Remember that when it's your turn."

His turn? He swallowed and looked at Claire.

"Something wrong?" she whispered.

He shook his head. "What's our baby girl's name?"

"Maggie. Jake picked it. It was Joanna's mother's name."

"Sounds perfect. Thanks for calling, Mom."

"She's coming home tomorrow. Can you believe that? They keep them only twenty-four hours now. Joanna and Jake said they'd stop by here on their way back to Wyattville. We'll have a late lunch together, a little welcome-home party for Maggie. Can you come, Sam? I know it's a long drive and you'd have to take off work, but it would mean so much to Jake and Joanna."

He could hardly wait to kiss Joanna and smoke a cigar with his brother. But could he leave Claire alone?

No doubt she wouldn't be alone for long. Pete watch-her-brush-off-her-ass Mission would probably be glad to get in the game. Tom Ames could be the backup quarterback.

Sam had always hated sitting on the sidelines.

"Hang on, Mom," he said. He held the receiver to his chest.

"Claire," he said, "my sister-in-law had her baby today and my mom wants to do some kind of family thing. I usually stay the night. It's short notice, but I'd want you to come, too. Do you think you could get off work tomorrow? We'd be back early enough Thursday for you to work a half day. Sound okay?"

"I…I guess. I have some personal days."

He lifted the receiver, readying himself for a modified Spanish Inquisition. "Mom, I can come, but I need to bring a friend."

"A friend?"

He could hear the little wheels in his mother's head start to turn. "Don't get excited, Mom. It's just Claire Fontaine. She had a little trouble at her apartment, so she's staying with me for a few days."

"Claire Fontaine." The wheels sounded as if they'd come to a grinding halt. His parents hadn't been happy when the Fontaines had thrown him to the wolves.

"It's no big deal. I'll tell you all about it when I get there," he said. "I'll see you then."

Sam hung up the phone. Claire remained at the end of the hall, staring at him.

"So we're set?" he said.

She shook her head, suddenly looking very weary. "I'm sorry. I just can't."

Chapter Seven

"Don't get excited, Mom. It's just Claire Fontaine. No big deal."

Like water dripping on a stone, his words battered her soul. She was just Claire. Which meant she was nothing to Sam Vernelli and she'd be well served to remember that.

Wait. That wasn't exactly true. She wasn't nothing. She was Tessa's sister.

Which was worse than being nothing.

She flopped down on the futon. And the tears, the ones she hadn't shed when her apartment had been burglarized or when there'd been a dead woman on her couch, they came with a vengeance, making her eyes burn and her head ache. She buried her face in her arms and pulled the pillow over her head.

Crying wasn't horrible. Having Sam Vernelli hear her crying was. He'd demand to know why and he wouldn't stop poking and prodding at her until she told him. And what could she say?

For some stupid reason, when you asked if I could go, I got excited about the idea that you wanted to spend time with me. Claire Fontaine. Just because I'm me. Not because I'm Tessa's little sister.

He'd think she was a nut. She wasn't sure he'd be wrong. Not for the first time, Claire wondered if it would have all been different if Tessa had lived. Would there have been Sunday dinners and late-night movies and family vacations? Would there have been joy? Would there have been love?

Would she have been able to pick up the phone, call up her mom and spill about how darn excited she was to be a finalist in the competition? Would she have been able to tease her dad that she actually had been listening all those years at the dinner table and had already enrolled in the retirement plan?

Would she send them a quick text, letting them know she'd eaten at a great restaurant, or seen a cool play or ridden the Ferris wheel at Navy Pier?

Would they have been more than polite acquaintances living in the same house?

Claire punched her pillow. What good did it do to wonder, to try to remember a time when there had been sunshine instead of shadows, warmth instead of cold, interest instead of apathy?

She couldn't change the past no matter how much she wanted to. All she could focus on was the future and what she could control. She closed her eyes and started making plans.

Three hours later, she woke up with a stiff neck, a dry throat and firm resolve. She had a list. One, move back to her apartment. Two, focus on the advertising competition. Three, forget the horrible telephone message, the dead woman on her couch and Sam Vernelli.

Simple.

In a month, this would be a dim memory. A you'll-never-believe-what-happened-to-me kind of story she could tell at her next cocktail party.

Like she ever went to cocktail parties.

She might, she reasoned, as she sat up and stretched her head from side to side, if she won the competition.

Right now, however, a thirty-dollar bottle of wine didn't interest her. She wanted water. She swung her legs off the futon, careful to avoid Nightmare, who dreamed happy dog-dreams at the end of the bed. She opened the bedroom door and silently walked to the kitchen. Fortunately for her, Sam had left one dim light burning above his sink.

She ran the water for a moment, letting it get cold. Then she filled a glass and drank it, not bothering to breathe between gulps. Then she refilled it and took the glass over to the table. Quietly, mindful that Sam slept, she unzipped her shoulder bag and pulled out a stack of unopened mail. The day had been so crazy that she'd taken her overflowing in-box and dumped it in her bag.

She was halfway through the pile when she opened a large white envelope and stuck her hand inside. She pulled out one sheet of plain paper, neatly folded. She flipped the paper open and bold, black slashes of pen jumped at her.

You're nothing special. But I do especially want to see you pay.

She jerked back, her knees bumped the table and her mostly empty plastic water glass hit the floor and rolled. She ignored it and stared at the paper.

Nightmare, evidently startled by the sudden noise in his kitchen, barked and Claire heard the unmistakable squeak of Sam's door. She knew she had mere seconds and she desperately wanted to pick up the paper, to rip it to shreds, to pretend that she'd never seen it.

"Claire?" Sam asked, his voice quiet. He stood in the doorway, his hair rumpled, wearing nothing but pajama pants low on his hips.

"I'm sorry I woke you," she said, trying hard to keep the

fear, the rage, the cacophony of emotions that the words caused out of her voice.

She evidently wasn't successful because his glance flicked around the room, taking in the still-bolted door, the spilled water, the stack of mail. He crossed the small space in four strides and squatted next to her.

"Claire, what's wrong?" he asked.

She pointed at the paper.

He stood up to read it. He was close enough that she could hear the quick intake of breath, could see the ripple of taut stomach muscle and could feel the instantaneous rage that consumed him.

"Where did this come from?" he demanded. He was pale and his eyes were wide and unfocused.

"I don't know," she said, insanely trying to defuse his tension and maybe even her own. She reached for the envelope and he grabbed her arm, his hand firm around her wrist.

"Don't touch it," he said.

His hand was warm and she swore that she could feel his energy radiating through the tips of his fingers. "Too late," she said. "I already touched it when I opened it."

He released her wrist and with the end of a pencil, he flipped the ten-by-thirteen envelope over. In the middle of it, Claire's first and last name was scrawled in black marker. The rest of the envelope was bare. There were no stamps on it, no post office markings.

"When did this come?" Sam asked.

"Today, I think."

He ran his hands through his thick hair, making it even messier than before. He sat down on the chair, his movements clumsy. She reached out to touch his arm. He jerked and stood up so suddenly that his chair went skidding behind him. Nightmare, lying in front of the refrigerator, barked in protest. Sam pointed to the paper, his movements sharp, abrupt.

"I've got to get this to the evidence techs. There might be prints, something, that will help us."

"Sam," she said, wrapping her arms around her middle. "It's the middle of the night."

"I know what time it is," he said, his voice sharp. He took three steps, yanked open the drawer next to the stove and pulled out two gallon-sized plastic bags. He grabbed a pair of tongs out of the white jar on the counter. He returned to the table and carefully, picking up just the edge of the letter and the envelope, put each into a separate bag.

He didn't look at her. She had the feeling that he'd prefer it if he never had to look at her again.

"Now what?" she asked, nodding her head at the plastic bags.

"We work the case." A look of real pain crossed his face. "Somebody wants to see you pay. For what, Claire?"

She shook her head. "I don't know. Honest to goodness, I don't know. Maybe it's just some creep who heard about what happened and is trying to scare me? Maybe it's the landlord's crazy brother?"

Sam's head snapped up. "The landlord has a crazy brother?"

"Maybe. I don't know. I'm just trying to make a point.

"There's no stamp, nothing to indicate the post office handled it. This is interoffice mail."

She'd come to the same conclusion and it was a chilling thought. She thought her coworkers liked her. Everybody was nice. She'd worked with the group for only four months. It was staggering to think that someone might hate her and even more appalling that they would come to that conclusion in such a short amount of time. "Do you think that everything is connected? That the robbery,

Sandy Bird, that awful telephone call and now this are all tangled up?"

He shook his head. "I don't know. Do people at your work know about the burglary and about Sandy Bird?"

"Hannah knows. Her cousin lives in my building. It's hard to know who she may have told."

"So, we have to assume that some people know. But what doesn't fit is that the caller knew something about Tessa's death that wasn't public information. How could anyone at your work have that knowledge?"

"I don't think they could."

"Me either. We have to consider that it might not be connected at all. Maybe it's somebody work, who has heard about your troubles and decided that your lemons are his or her lemonade."

"Huh?"

"It's the equivalent of the playground pile-on. One of your coworkers isn't a fan and has been secretly celebrating your misfortune. It gives him or her courage to express his own thoughts. It's the little kid taunting the other kid, *See, nobody likes you.*"

"Who would do that?"

"I don't know. But you're not going to work today. You're going to my parents' house with me," Sam said. "Tell your boss you need the day off."

"I'm busy at work."

"Bring it with you." He pointed to the stack of mail. "Looks like you're pretty used to that."

She wanted to argue, wanted to pretend that she had better things to do. But truth be told, the letter, on top of the phone message, on top of everything else that had happened, had her freaked out.

She might not like being told what to do, but she wasn't stupid. "What time do we leave?" she asked.

"Early morning. I should be back in plenty of time."

"Back?"

"Yeah. I'm taking this in. Right now. We're running out of time to find answers."

SAM AND CLAIRE LEFT the apartment shortly after seven the next morning. Sam was dressed in jeans and a plaid flannel shirt and he carried a thermos of coffee and a whole lot of attitude. Claire wore a gray midcalf corduroy skirt, black boots and a raspberry-colored lightweight sweater. She wanted the coffee and had more than enough of her own attitude.

Sam had had less than three hours of sleep. She knew that because she'd been awake when he'd come home. It had been another hour before she'd managed to shut down. Even Nightmare had looked a little cross with her tossing-and-turning routine.

When she'd stumbled into the kitchen shortly after six, Sam had been sitting at the table. He'd mumbled "Good morning" and shoved a box of cereal in her direction, before taking off for the shower. He'd never once looked at her.

She'd managed to push a few bites down, all the time wondering what the heck she was doing. She didn't have to go to Sam's parents' house. She didn't have to spend the day trying to ignore the furtive whispers or the wondering looks as his family searched for but found no resemblance to Tessa. She'd met the Vernellis just once, at Tessa's funeral. She remembered them as quiet, polite people who were shocked by Tessa's death. She remembered Sam standing over Tessa's grave, long after the service had ended. Everyone else was making their way back to their cars. His mother had turned, walked back to her son, wrapped an arm around his shoulders and led him away from the grave.

Now, as he pulled his shiny red SUV up to the curb, she willed her legs to run. But just then, the bright morning sun bounced off the hood of the vehicle, crossed his strong features and caught the hint of pain in his dark eyes. And she knew she couldn't do it.

She pulled open the door and slid in, noting that Nightmare, in the backseat, wedged between Sam's duffel bag and her suitcase, looked the happiest.

She shoved her laptop case onto the floor and rested her feet on it. "Nice day," she said, determined to try.

He didn't answer.

"Perfect day for a high school football game."

He looked at her. "You had plans to go to a football game?"

"No," she said, her face feeling hot. "Just making conversation."

He turned, facing forward again. "Right."

Yeah, right. She stayed silent while he navigated the city streets, but traffic was light and soon they were flying along on the highway headed for Minnesota.

An hour out of the city, lulled into sleepiness by the warmth of the sun on her face, she drifted off. Later, she didn't know if it was ten minutes or two hours, Sam gently shook her shoulder.

"Claire," he said, his tone soft, like he didn't want to scare her. "You need to wake up."

She opened her eyes, blinking them fast. "We're here?" she asked, stretching her aching neck.

"No," he said. He stared at her, not smiling, but his tone seemed gentler than before. "I need to let Nightmare out to do his thing. I didn't want to leave you alone in the car asleep."

Of course not. Careful Detective Vernelli would want her awake and aware. While she'd thought she might enjoy sleeping for another couple hours, she appreciated the fact that he seemed determined to keep her safe.

"No problem," she said. Sam had pulled into a highway rest stop. There was a large, grassy area and a small, neat brick building that she assumed offered restrooms. "I think I'll go inside myself," she said, reaching for the door handle.

Sam looked around the parking lot. She did the same. Five cars and two semis. Looked safe enough to her. Must have to him as well because he nodded. "Okay. I'll meet you inside in a few minutes."

She grabbed her purse, pushed open the door and headed inside. The restrooms were surprisingly neat and when she finished, she drifted over to the brochure rack that covered one side of the lobby wall. She'd skimmed most of them by the time Sam came inside.

She saw him, flashed a quick smile, and stuffed one of the brochures in her purse. Not quick enough, however, to avoid Sam's eagle eye.

"What's that?" he asked.

She pulled it out and handed it to him.

"Canoeing?" he asked, cocking his head to one side. "You like to canoe?"

She shrugged. "I don't know. I've never done it."

He frowned at her. "Never?"

"My parents weren't crazy about my trying anything that had any potential for danger."

"What?" He looked puzzled, but then he sighed and shook his head. "Everybody copes in a different way."

"I guess. Anyway, I have wanted to try it for years. Maybe I can work it in yet this fall. If not, then next spring for sure."

He handed her back the brochure. "That's a good place," he said. "I've done their trips. They range from three hours to three days."

"Three days? Yikes. That would be two nights of sleeping outside?"

He laughed and suddenly looked years younger. "Oh, yeah. No extra charge for the mosquitoes."

"Great. I love a good value."

"Come on," he said, wrapping an arm around her shoulder, "let's go before Nightmare eats the seat cushions. If I'm right, Mom's pulling the fresh-baked coffee cake out of the oven right now. Hope you're not philosophically opposed to sugar."

"Uh, no," she replied as she almost tripped. Having Sam's arm around her shoulder made it difficult to walk or talk. Not that it meant anything to him.

"How much farther?" she asked as they reached the car.

Sam took his arm away and used it to open her door. "We'll be there in an hour. Can't wait to see the little rug rat."

Claire slid in and smiled at Nightmare who had his head hanging over the front seat. "How long have your brother and sister-in-law been married?" she asked, once Sam got in.

"About a year. I think they were both anxious to start a family."

"How did they meet?"

Sam smiled. "Well, it's sort of a funny story. Now, that is. At the time, it was pretty tense. Joanna, known as Tara then, was hiding in Wyattville. Living under an assumed name, living a life totally different than the one she'd had to leave before her sorry-excuse-for-a-man ex-fiancé made good on his promise to kill her. Jake was doing some interim duty as the police chief, helping out an old friend.

Short story is he managed to get the guy and the girl. He got damn lucky on both counts."

"Do they still live in Wyattville?"

"Yes. Joanna has a little restaurant there. Works her tail off. Maybe a baby will slow her down a little."

"Does Jake work at the restaurant, too?"

"No. The interim job turned into a full-time gig."

She frowned at him. "I thought I remembered my mother saying once that your father was a police officer."

"He was. Guess it's in our blood. We all seem to like it pretty well." He backed the car out of its parking space. "How about you? You like your job?"

Getting the anonymous letter at work had left a bad taste in her mouth, but yes, she loved her job. Loved the opportunity to be creative every day, to talk to customers, to offer new ways to advertise their products. "Yes. I'm incredibly lucky to be working at a top agency."

"They knew talent when they saw it."

Oh, man. "I guess I work pretty hard to make sure that I earn the right to work there."

"So, do you work closely with that guy you were sitting on the steps with? Mission, right?"

"Some. I did my first big market-research project with Pete and I learned so much."

"I'll bet."

Claire swiveled in her seat, pulling on her seat belt. Sam faced forward, his eyes scanning the road, looking like he didn't have a care in the world. Then she noticed the grip he had on the steering wheel. His knuckles were almost white. "He lives in a very nice neighborhood," Sam said.

"Hannah said that his parents died when he was in his early twenties. That was their house."

"Is he married?" Sam asked, surprising her.

"No. I'm sure he dates. He doesn't say much about it."

"So how old do you think he is?" Sam asked, his tone casual, too casual.

Why was Sam so fascinated with Pete? "Why? Are you interested in him?" She knew it was a ridiculous question, but Sam was acting very weird.

Sam gave her a look that told her he didn't think she was funny. "Oh, fine," she said. "I guess about forty. I don't really know."

Sam shrugged. "He's way too old for you."

"What?"

Sam shrugged and faced forward again. "I just think you need to be careful around men like that?"

What the heck was he talking about? "Men like what?"

He tapped one finger against the steering wheel. "Never mind."

"No way. Don't say something like that and then just shut down."

He checked both mirrors, flipped on his signal and switched lanes. They drove another half mile and with each turn of the tires, Claire could practically feel her blood pressure rising. Finally, she couldn't take it anymore. "Look, Sam. When two people have a conversation, it's helpful if they both talk."

He let out an audible puff of air. "Fine. When a guy looks at a girl's butt the way he was looking at yours, I don't think he's really all that interested in doing business. Unless his business is focused around getting some on the conference-room table."

A vision of skinny Pete Mission with his pants around his ankles leaning her backward over the polished cherrywood table made her want to howl.

"Well?" Sam prodded. He looked so serious and it made Claire work extra hard to keep from laughing. She turned her head toward the window, buying time until she could get it under control.

"Claire," he said, his voice husky. "I'm a jerk. That was crude. There are probably ten ways I could have said that better. I'm sorry."

He thought she was offended. That was even funnier. She was just about to let him in on the joke when he leaned over and placed his hand on her knee. Her leg, the stupid, traitorous limb it was, jerked, just like Nightmare's rump did when Claire petted it. Sam's hand felt firm and capable and she could feel the heat all the way through her skirt.

She really needed to get the upper hand here before she did something crazy like grab his hand and stick it down her shirt. She turned toward Sam and gave him her best wide-eyed, don't-have-a-clue look. "Do you really think that's what he's interested in? You think he wants to…to *sleep* with me?"

Sam's neck turned red, matching the plaid in his shirt. "I'm just saying," he said, his voice sounding strangled, "that you need to be careful."

Claire waved her hand. "Oh, we'd be careful. There's a lock on the conference-room door."

Sam's truck swerved and Claire heard the satisfying sound of tires on loose gravel as Sam brought the vehicle back on the highway. "That's not what I meant," he said.

"You think we should leave the door open?" she said, her voice deliberately shocked.

Sam glanced at her, his mouth open.

"So people could *watch?*" she asked, cocking her head to the side, like some stuffed dog in the window of an old lady's car.

Sam shut his mouth and narrowed his eyes. With a sudden movement, he flipped on his signal, pressed on the brake and pulled the car far off the highway, almost into the short, yellow-green grass. When the car had stopped, he turned in his seat. "You're yanking my chain, aren't you?" he said, his voice soft.

"I just can't help but wonder," she said, "do outrageous things just fall out of your mouth or do you have to work at it?"

He held up a finger and pointed it at her. "Laugh all you want. He wasn't happy about my being at his house the other night. That tells me that he's got a thing for you."

She rolled her eyes. "Even if you're right, which you're not, but if you are, I can handle Pete Mission."

Now she could see the anger flashing in his eyes. He leaned over toward her and gently grabbed her chin. "I've investigated more than my share of sexually violent attacks against women," he said, his voice stern. "It's not pretty and it sure as hell isn't something to laugh about. Most of these attacks are perpetrated by somebody the victim knows. So don't assume anybody is harmless."

He was so close. She could feel the heat coming off his body. His lips were just inches away. She licked her lips and then his grip around her chin tightened, not enough to hurt, but just enough that she knew he felt the connection as much as she did. Oh, man. Sam Vernelli shouldn't be worrying about her virtue or safety; he should be worrying about his own.

"I'm sorry," she said, pulling away. She couldn't think when he was touching her. "I got carried away at your expense."

He let his hand drop back into his lap. "You had me going," he admitted. "The watching thing was a little over the top. That's what did you in."

"Watching isn't your thing?" she asked, suddenly feeling bold.

He stared at her, not blinking, maybe not even breathing. "I prefer to participate," he said finally. Then he shook his head, like he couldn't believe what he'd just said. "I should not be having this conversation with you."

With you—Tessa's sister. He didn't need to say it. The meaning was clear enough.

"Well," she said, looking straight ahead, "because you're into participation, when we're a man short on our volleyball team, at least we know who to call."

Sam started the car. After he'd pulled out onto the highway, Claire risked a look at him. His jaw was set, his lips pressed together and he looked mad as hell.

She didn't know if he was mad at her or himself. She didn't think it probably mattered.

Chapter Eight

Sam, with Nightmare dancing around his heels, yanked open the back door of his parents' house. "Shouldn't we knock?" Claire asked, more certain than ever this was a mistake.

Sam frowned at her. "I used to live here," he said. "Come on. Something smells good."

At least he was talking again. He'd barely spoken for the last hour of the trip. Claire let him lead her down the wide, ceramic-tiled hallway into a large blue-and-white kitchen with oak cabinets and a big, round, pedestal-style oak table in the center.

Mrs. Vernelli had her back to them, bending over an open oven door. Her husband stood next to her, stirring a pot of something, while he stared out the kitchen window, focused on the small yellow birds that were hopping on and off the bird feeder that hung on a backyard tree. Ten feet away, through the wide archway that led to the family room, an absolutely gorgeous woman sat on the couch next to a slightly older, leaner version of Sam. The man held the woman's hand and they both stared into the bassinet that was trimmed with yellow and green ribbons.

"Hey," Sam said, loud enough to get some attention but not so loud as to wake a sleeping baby. "What's for lunch?"

Mrs. Vernelli whirled around, both hands firmly

gripped around a roasting pan. She stared first at her youngest son and then at Claire. She opened her mouth but no words came out. The woman's slightly plump cheeks were pink and Claire didn't know if it was from the heat of the oven, the pleasure of seeing her youngest son or the shock of seeing Tessa's little sister in her kitchen. To her credit, Mrs. Vernelli recovered quickly and offered them one of the most genuinely warm smiles that Claire had ever seen.

She set down the roasting pan and crossed the room. Standing on her tiptoes, she hugged Sam. Then she extended her arm and shook Claire's hand. "Claire. It's good to see you again. I'm so glad you could come."

"It was kind of you to include me," she said.

Mr. Vernelli, who had put down his spoon, waved his hand as if it was nothing. Perhaps Sam routinely dragged women home. "I'm Tom. We were sorry to hear about the trouble at your apartment, Claire. Your parents must be very concerned."

"Yes, of course," she said, thinking she better tell her parents soon. She took a second glance at Tom Vernelli. He had twenty-five years on Sam, but his still-handsome face had the same strong bone structure, his eyes danced with the same keen intelligence.

"How are your folks?" Mrs. Vernelli asked.

"Busy." It was the standard answer. The week before she'd left for Chicago, her mother had been named Volunteer of the Year by a local group. They'd all gone to the awards dinner. It had been a painful reminder of how far apart she and her mother had grown. When the presenter had read off the list of organizations that her mother supported, Claire hadn't recognized more than half. She'd wanted to ask her father, but he'd been out in the hall, cell phone to his ear, negotiating the purchase of another company.

"So, do I get to see my niece?" Sam asked, edging toward the bassinet. He bent down and brushed a kiss across the woman's forehead and then roughly hugged his brother who'd stood up. Claire was struck by the resemblance between the two men. Both tall and handsome as heck.

"Claire," Sam said. "This gorgeous creature is my sister-in-law, Joanna. The big oaf next to her is my brother, Jake."

Both of them flashed a smile, but she didn't miss that Jake's gaze was a little more assessing, a little more curious.

"How's she doing?" Sam asked, pointing at the bassinet.

"Take a look for yourself," Joanna said, her voice warm with maternal pride. She shifted and leaned toward the bassinet. When she winced, her husband put his hand on her arm.

"Let me," he said. Then the man carefully reached his big hands into the bassinet and lifted out the baby. She was swaddled in a soft yellow blanket. When he made a motion to hand the sweet bundle to his brother, Sam backed up a step. "No, you hold her," Sam said. "I'll break her."

Joanna laughed. "No, you won't."

"You don't know that," Sam said, sounding very serious. He looked at Claire and she thought it might be real panic that she saw on his face. "Help me out, here, okay?" he said. He looked back to his brother. "Give her to Claire."

Jake rolled his eyes and then carefully, very carefully, placed the precious bundle in her curved arms. She stared at the round little face, the wisps of strawberry-blond hair and the rosebud mouth, and fell instantly and thoroughly in love. "Oh, she's perfect," she said.

And then Sam came close and bent his head. Cautiously, he took one finger and lifted the edge of the blanket away from the baby's face. He stared for a minute, then looked up at Jake. "You did good," he said, his voice soft.

Jake looked at his wife, his eyes filled with love. "I did nothing," he said. "Joanna did it all."

"He had the fun part," Joanna replied, her tone dry.

Mr. and Mrs. Vernelli, their arms wrapped around each other's back, laughed. Mr. Vernelli winked at his wife of many years and she blushed like a young woman.

Claire felt a little piece of her heart break. This was what a family should be. People who loved, fiercely and proudly. And to her utter embarrassment, her eyes filled with tears. She tried to blink them away, but Sam, the observant fool he was, saw her.

"Hey," he said, "what's wrong?"

Claire looked around the room. Sam's father, who obviously felt ill at ease with a woman's tears, fidgeted, shifting his weight from foot to foot. His mother, her eyes an equal mixture of question and concern, stared at her. Jake, chewing his bottom lip, turned to Joanna, who shrugged her delicate shoulders. Claire settled her glance on Sam. His eyes were filled with something she couldn't define, but it warmed her soul, like the sun shining through the car window had warmed her face. "I'm just so happy," she said, her voice thick with tears, "for all of you."

An awkward silence hung in the air and Claire wished she could sink into the floor. Then Joanna, her eyes suddenly full of understanding, patted the couch next to her. "Come sit next to me. We'll admire the baby together and let the men wait on us."

"Why should today be any different?" Mr. Vernelli asked and then made a big production of protecting his head, like he expected his wife to swing a cast iron skillet. Sam and Jake laughed and as easily as that, the moment passed. Claire, careful not to jostle the baby, sank down on the couch.

"Thank you," she whispered to Joanna.

"You'll get used to it," Joanna whispered back. "It can be a bit overwhelming at first."

"You got that right," Claire said, rocking the baby gently in her arms. She watched while Jake began to unload the dishwasher and Sam, grabbing milk and butter in one hand and an electric mixer in the other, approached the steaming pan of boiled potatoes. "They really fill up a kitchen," she said.

Joanna wrinkled her nose. "Nothing sexier than a man in an apron."

Claire had a quick and fleeting vision of Sam wearing nothing but an apron. "Uh, yes," she managed.

"Imagine this," Joanna said, winking at her. "The first time I saw the two of them together, they were playing basketball. With their shirts off. It was ninety degrees outside, they were sweating, and I was drooling. It was quite an event."

"Do you think they know?" Claire whispered, studying Sam and Jake as they completed their tasks.

"I suspect they do," Joanna said. "It's just not important to them. By the way, does Sam know you're interested?"

She thought about denying it, but knew she wasn't that good of an actress. "It wouldn't dawn on him. I'm Tessa's little sister."

"I'm sorry about your sister," Joanna said. "It must have been horrible. But it was a long time ago. She and Sam were very young."

Claire bit her lower lip. "I'm pretty sure he's still in love with her."

Joanna's pretty green eyes shifted to Sam. He had finished mashing the potatoes and was now scooping out big spoonfuls into a yellow bowl. His mother stood at his side, supervising. When he pretended to stick a finger into the potatoes, his mother whacked his shoulder with a wooden spoon. Joanna smiled and shrugged. "He wouldn't have brought you here if he didn't have feelings—"

"Food's ready," Mrs. Vernelli interrupted. She stood next to the table and gestured for them to come.

Joanna reached for the baby and then gently laid her down in the bassinet. "For you," she finished.

THE BABY SLEPT through lunch, awakening just as Sheryl Vernelli cleared off the last dessert plates. When Maggie let out a little squawk, Jake's and Sam's heads swiveled, like they were ready to spring into immediate action. Joanna, looking infinitely more relaxed, pushed her chair back, calmly walked over to the bassinet and lifted the crying baby out of her crib. The two of them settled in the padded rocking chair in the corner of the large family room and Joanna discreetly raised the corner of her shirt.

Jake watched for a minute and then, apparently satisfied that all was well, made a big production out of standing up and patting his full stomach. "Dad," he said, "I've misplaced my needle-nose pliers. You wouldn't happen to have an extra pair?"

Tom Vernelli scratched his chin. "I'm not sure, Son. Why don't I take a walk out to the garage with you and we'll look."

Jake nodded and looked pointedly at Sam. "Sam, have you checked on your dog lately?"

"Uh, no. That's a good idea," Sam added. He pushed his chair back from the table. When he walked past his mom, he kissed her forehead. "Just leave the dishes. Jake and I'll handle them." When he walked past Claire's chair, he put a hand on her shoulder. Light. Impersonal. And she felt the heat down to her toes.

"You doing okay?" he asked.

"Stuffed," she said, desperately trying to focus on her stomach and ignore the strength and masculine feel of his large hand. His nails were trimmed short and, if she wasn't mistaken, his little finger had been broken at least once.

"You got up early after a pretty late night," he said. "Why don't you try to snag a nap?"

She turned her face up and her eyes met his. "You got less sleep than I did," she reminded him.

"I guess that's true," he said. He looked very serious. He stared at her for several seconds and the kitchen suddenly seemed very quiet. Then he smiled. "I'll wrestle you for the couch later," he said. He lifted his hand off her shoulder and patted the top of her head.

Like he did to Nightmare every time the darn dog walked by.

In a clatter of bootheels on ceramic tile, the Vernelli men left. The quiet in the kitchen was absolute except the occasional gentle slurping from the rocking chair. Sheryl Vernelli motioned for Claire to follow her into the family room. The older woman took the corner of the green couch and Claire settled into the overstuffed brown leather chair.

Joanna looked up from her baby and flashed a smile. "You'll have to forgive them. They simply can't stop being cops."

Mrs. Vernelli coughed into her hand and smiled. Claire decided she hadn't liked anyone as immediately as Joanna in a long time. "Thanks. I appreciate your not pretending that they're not out there discussing me."

Mrs. Vernelli picked up a book off the table next to her, thumbed the pages, then put the book back down. "I must say," she offered, somewhat hesitantly, "I haven't seen Sam this serious for a long time. He's normally full of jokes."

It seemed like she'd barely seen him smile. "I guess he'll be relieved when I'm out of his hair."

"I suppose," said Mrs. Vernelli as she picked up the hardcover book one more time and tapped her nail against the spine. It reminded Claire of how Sam rubbed the tips of his index finger and his thumb together when he was nervous.

What in heavens did Mrs. Vernelli have to be nervous about?

CLAIRE WOKE UP when Nightmare jumped on top of her. "Hey, you big lug," she said, pulling her arm from beneath the warm yellow comforter to rub the dog's fur.

He started to turn in circles. She knew what that meant. She had about two minutes before he started to howl. She didn't want him to wake the baby. "Oh, fine. I'll take you out."

She swung her legs over the edge of the bed. It couldn't be much past dawn and the house had cooled down during the night. She opened her suitcase and pulled out blue jeans and a sweatshirt. She quickly stepped out of her pajamas and into her clothes. She ran a hand through her hair. Her brush was in her purse and she'd left that downstairs.

"Let's go," she said, opening the door. "Be quiet," she warned, as the dog zoomed past her. No doubt everyone else in the house would still be sleeping.

When they got to the back door, Claire slipped Nightmare's leash onto his collar. They left the house and she was really glad she'd worn her sweatshirt. Good Lord, it was cold enough that she could see her breath. She pulled the hood of her sweatshirt up and stuck the hand that didn't hold Nightmare's leash into her jeans pocket.

She and Nightmare walked around the yard until Nightmare found a spot to do his thing. When the dog finished, she rubbed his head. "You're a good boy," she said. "You really had to go, didn't you?"

Nightmare thumped his tail, looking proud. "What do you say we take a walk, sweetie?" She rubbed her fingers across the dollar bills in her pocket and knew she had enough for coffee. If she remembered correctly, there was a gas station-slash-convenience store on the corner, about two blocks away. She pulled gently on Nightmare's chain, but the dog yanked his head the other direction and let out two sharp barks.

Claire looked and she could see Sam, dressed in dark blue warm-up pants and a gray sweatshirt running toward her. His arms were pumping, his legs flying, and it made her heart start thumping.

Slow down, Sam. Let me enjoy the view.

Still a block away, he held up his arm, letting her know that he'd seen her. She watched his big body move toward her and her mouth felt dry. My, my, he was a fine specimen of a man.

"Morning," she said, when he got close enough to hear. She hoped her voice sounded more casual than she felt. With his hair ruffled by the wind, his cheeks red from the cold and his chest heaving up and down in flat-out exhaustion, he made her cold body feel warm in certain spots.

"Good morning," he answered, his hands braced on his thighs as he struggled for breath. He straightened up and walked around her in circles, no doubt getting his heart rate to slow down.

What was she going to do about hers?

"How far did you run?" she asked.

"About five miles."

"All at that pace?"

He shook his head, almost looking embarrassed. "I was a sprinter in high school. Over the years, I've learned to slow it down so I can increase my distance, but I still love it when I can relive my youth."

She wrapped her arms around her middle. "You say that like you're in your eighties."

"I'm almost thirty-three. There's a big difference between that and seventeen."

"I guess."

He studied her. "You know, that makes me close to nine years older than you."

What was his point?

"We're at different stages of our lives," he added, his breathing steadier now.

"What stage are you in?" she asked, really wanting to know. Sam was a master at not talking about himself.

"That's not important," he said, disappointing her. "What is important is that you're in your early twenties. You've got plenty of time before you need to be thinking about things."

"Things?"

He waved a hand. "Like marriage and babies. I mean," he said, "it's not like you're Joanna's age. She's past thirty and just having her first baby. That's pretty common these days."

"I suppose." She looked away.

He stepped to the side so that she was once again looking at him. "Did I say something wrong?"

"I'm cold," she said. "I'm going in."

She got two steps before he gently grabbed her arm and turned her to face him. "Please tell me," he said.

"I guess I just get tired of your being so focused on age, especially my age. It's a number, okay? That's all it is." She tightened the strings of her hood, hiding more of her face. He was looking at her so intently that it was like he was looking into her soul.

"I'm sorry," he said. He wrapped an arm around her shoulder and pulled her tight against his chest. He felt warm and solid and he smelled like fresh air and sweaty male.

He shifted her in his arms until she was standing in front of him. He pushed back the sides of her hood and with two fingers under her chin, tilted her head up. "Let's talk about something else. The other night, when I picked you up at Mission's house, you said that you had both been nominated for an award. Tell me about it."

"It's a design contest, sponsored by the Chicago Advertising Association. I guess it's a pretty big deal. The grand-prize winner walks away with a $15,000 check."

He pulled back. "What are your chances?"

"There are six finalists, so I guess statistically, I have a little over a 15 percent chance of winning. But in reality, it's a lot less. I'm sure I have the least experience of any of the finalists. Their designs are probably much better."

"What does Mission's design look like?"

She shook her head. "I don't know. Several of us from the agency entered, but none of us shared our designs. In our business, we do a lot of brainstorming. Somebody comes up with an idea and then everybody throws out suggestions, building upon the original idea. It's just how we're wired. But in this particular contest, entrants have to sign a statement that they haven't collaborated with anyone—that the design is solely their own creation. I guess none of us wanted to accidentally step over the line."

"When will you know who won?"

"Not until the awards dinner on Monday. Most everyone from the agency is going to attend." She rubbed her hands together. "Come on, let's go inside. Even Nightmare looks cold."

"Come on," he said, gathering up Nightmare's leash. "I'm betting Mom has coffee started by now and Dad's probably mixing up the pancake batter."

"Are his pancakes as good as yours?"

"No, but don't let him know that."

Chapter Nine

Sam and Claire left right after breakfast and were back in Chicago by noon. Claire was in her bedroom changing into work clothes when she heard Sam's cell phone ring.

She finished zipping her dress and walked out of the room. Sam was filling Nightmare's water dish and listening to the person on the other end. "Where?" he asked. Then more listening. "Okay, thanks, Cruz. I'll let Claire know and ask her if the description rings a bell." He hung up.

"Let Claire know what?" she asked.

"Some of your stuff turned up at a pawnshop north of downtown. Little place on Sheraton Road. Had the television and one of the necklaces."

"What was that about a description?"

"Owner said it was a woman. About twenty-five, with brown eyes and curly, short hair the same color. Also, he said she acted like she knew the drill, like she'd been in a pawnshop before. Anybody you know?"

"Short, brown hair. Brown eyes. Sounds like he could have been describing me. Except for the part that she knew her way around a pawnshop. I've never been in one."

"You're not missing much," he said.

"I'm sorry," she said, feeling disappointed. She wanted this to be over. "I guess I'm not much help."

"Not much help? You had a serial number for the television. That's amazing. I think you might be the only person in America who regularly records the serial numbers of their electronics."

She heard the mocking tone and didn't know if he was making fun of her or deliberately trying to lighten the mood. "I organize my office supplies, too," she said. "Alphabetically. Binder clips in front and Zippo pens in the back."

He shifted his gaze and studied her. Frowning, he shook his head. "Just alpha? Not cross-referenced by function?"

So he had been teasing. "Don't tell anyone," she said, "but my underwear has the days of the week and once—" she dropped her voice to a whisper "—I wore Tuesday on a Sunday."

His lips made a small round circle. "And the Underwear Police still haven't found you?"

She shook her head. "I suppose," she said, unable to totally ignore Cruz's information, no matter how much she wanted to, "that this is a good thing. You know, it's a clue."

"Absolutely. I don't understand why you're not happier. You can get some of your things back."

"It's hard to explain," she said. She walked into the living room and sat down on the leather couch that bore the evidence of Nightmare's nails. "If the robbery really was connected to Sandy Bird, I don't know how I'm ever going to look at that television again and not think about how she looked after…"

"Oh, Claire," Sam said, and before she even knew what he was doing, he'd crossed the room and sat next to her. He wrapped an arm around her shoulder and pulled her toward him. She leaned in and laid her face against the softness of his T-shirt.

"At night," she said, "I close my eyes and it's a replay of

everything that happened. Of my walking into the living room and seeing Nadine and the woman. Of her, waving the gun at us. I thought I was going to die. I really did."

"It's okay, sweetheart," he crooned and rocked her back and forth. "You're safe with me."

She needed to tell him all of it. "When Nadine shot her, I couldn't believe it. I just sat there and stared and then I got sick. I didn't think I was ever going to stop vomiting. It was just so horrible. Sometimes I think I'm going crazy because I can almost smell her, smell the sweat, the cigarettes, the craziness that radiated from her."

Now the tears ran freely down her face and her body shook. Sam tightened his grip and gently patted her back with one hand.

"Then the phone call and the letter the other night. I guess I've been relying on the fact that I was sure the woman had picked us by accident. But now, I don't know. What if it wasn't random? Nadine killed her. She's going to have to live with that. And maybe she had to do it all because of me."

"I'm going to figure this out," Sam whispered. "I promise. You're not going to have to spend the rest of your life wondering. I'm going to find the link."

His body felt warm and hard and she desperately wanted to believe that he was doing it for her and not out of some crazy sense of honor. She pulled back and Sam immediately released her.

"I know," she said, "that I'm going to have to go back to that apartment and look at my things and get on with my life."

"There's no hurry," he said, frowning at her. "You can stay with me. Watch my television."

She'd love that. But when it came time to leave, it would

be that much harder. She'd miss him all the more. "We'll see," she said.

"It's no problem," he assured her and then, ever so gently, with the pad of his thumb, he brushed the tears off her cheeks. At that moment, when she felt his strength, his courage, his infinite goodness, she knew she was in big trouble. She really liked Sam Vernelli. And to him, all she'd ever be was little Claire, Tessa's baby sister.

"I'm not generally a crier," she said, suddenly at a loss for words. "All evidence to the contrary."

He gave her a sweet, sexy smile. "I hate, absolutely hate, seeing you cry, but I think you probably deserve to shed a few tears." He reached out and held her hand. She felt the heat run up her arm. "You've been so brave, so strong," he added.

He thought she was brave. She wanted to be. Thought maybe she wouldn't get many more chances. She reached up and ran her fingers across Sam's jaw line. His skin felt rough, with the hint of whiskers. He didn't pull away, but his quick, almost-imperceptible shiver told her he might not be immune to her. "I like you, Sam," she said.

He bit his lower lip and his eyes became guarded. "I like you, too. You're a great kid."

Kid. This wasn't going to get them anywhere fast.

She needed to be bold. "I want to kiss you."

She heard his quick exhale of breath through his nose like he'd been punched in the stomach. "You're mixing gratitude with attraction," he said, his voice sounding strained. "It happens all the time. Cops are trained to recognize it."

Be bold. Be brave. "Oh, really?" She ran her finger across his lower lip. He remained absolutely still, like he was afraid to move. So she leaned forward, until she was close enough to see the flecks of gold in his brown eyes.

"Claire," he said, his voice a mere whisper.

She heard the plea in his tone and knew that it was a request to stop, but recklessly, like a child flying a kite in an approaching storm, she ignored it. And when she pressed her lips to his and her breasts up against his chest, lightning struck. A great gust of wind left his body and in one swift motion, he shifted so that she was no longer sitting up but was lying on her back, with him on top of her. He pressed his body into her and she could feel his strength, his power, his need.

She made him want. The raw glory of it surged through her.

And when he angled his head and stuck his tongue in her mouth, she soared. It was deep, delicious, delightful.

And she wanted him to kiss her forever.

When he finally did pull back, he reared up, his arms holding his weight off her body. He was breathing hard, his breath coming out in quick spurts followed by swift intake, like he might be on the verge of hyperventilating.

Oh, baby, she'd made him pant.

"Claire," he said, his voice cracking, making her name sound as if it had two syllables. "I...uh...I..."

Oh, yeah. She'd made him speechless.

"I've been wanting to do that for days," she said, shifting a little, trying to ease him back down. She couldn't budge him.

"That's impossible," he said, looking stricken.

She could feel his retreat. *Be bold.* She squirmed, pressing her pubic bone up, softly grinding her strength against his. He was hard. Very.

He jerked off her, almost flinging himself off the couch. He landed on the floor in a squatting position. He held up a hand. "We have got to stop this," he said. "It's not right."

She felt like she was being scolded like some naughty

child. She needed to make him understand. "Sam, I'm attracted to you. You need to know—"

"What I know," he said, his face red, "is that I'm responsible for you. And what just happened here was damned irresponsible."

"I never asked you to take responsibility for me," she said, her chest hurting. "I don't want you protecting me or shielding me." Her parents had practically smothered her—she sure as heck didn't intend to have that kind of relationship with Sam. "I haven't asked you to do anything for me. You don't owe me anything."

"I owe," he said. "I owe." His face had turned to stone and his eyes held the same miserable look they had each time he'd talked about Tessa. The meaning was clear enough. His debt was to Tessa. And nothing else mattered. She was Tessa's little sister. She'd get his protection whether she wanted it or not. But she wouldn't get anything else from him. Tessa had taken everything he had to give.

"You've been under stress," he said. "Things happening at home, at work. It's a lot to handle."

He seemed to want to give her a thousand excuses for why she'd thrown herself at him. Like he couldn't accept that it had been real—that what she felt could possibly be real.

Could she feel any more stupid?

"You're right," she lied. She stood up, glad that her legs would hold her. She took short, jerky steps over to the hallway table. She grabbed her purse, opened the door and left. She didn't say goodbye.

Sam had two thoughts as he watched her go. One, he was too stupid to live and two, it would take him a hundred years to forget Claire's scent. It hovered in the air, teasing him, making him want to sniff like a dog in heat. Citrus had always meant oranges. He'd been okay with that. Now it would mean sun-kissed skin, pretty eyes and soft lips.

When she'd been under him and she'd wrapped her bare legs around him, pulling him tight, it had been the most intense pleasure he'd ever felt. And the only right thing to do was forget about it.

He looked around, desperate to think about something else, and saw the sack lunch that she'd packed before she'd gone into the spare room to change into her work clothes. She'd packed it because they hadn't stopped for lunch on the way back. They were both full from breakfast and she'd been anxious to get back to work by noon. When she'd been spreading peanut butter and jelly on the bread, she'd said that it would be her three o'clock snack, that it would hold her over in the event that she decided to work later than usual.

Hell. She'd probably bust her chops until late tonight and do most of it on an empty stomach.

Not his problem.

He wondered if Pete look-at-her-ass Mission would be working late, too.

Not his concern.

He poured a big bowl of cereal and filled it to the rim with milk. "Don't give me that look," he scolded Nightmare. The dog put a paw over his only ear, like he couldn't bear to hear the story. "Hey, she kissed me," Sam said, his mouth full.

Right before he'd pressed her into the couch and every curve, every damn curve in her compact little body, had slid into place, fitting with his, like fine tongue-and-groove flooring. Sweet.

When she'd pressed up against him, he'd stopped thinking. Sort of like the night Micky Rivaci's switchblade had sliced into him and he'd teetered between life and death. He'd forced his mind blank and focused on nothing but

OFFICIAL OPINION POLL

Dear Reader,

Since you are a book enthusiast, we would like to know what you think.

Inside you will find a short Opinion Poll. Please participate in our poll by sharing your opinion on 3 subjects that are very important to all of us.

To thank you for your participation, we would like to send you **2 FREE BOOKS** and **2 FREE GIFTS!**

Please enjoy them with our compliments.

Sincerely,

Pam Powers

For Your Reading Pleasure...

Get 2 FREE BOOKS that feature
stories mixing breathtaking romance
with heart-stopping
suspense.

Your **2 FREE BOOKS** have a combined
cover price of $10.50 in the U.S. and
$12.50 in Canada.

◄ Peel off sticker and place by your
completed poll on the right page
and you'll automatically receive
2 FREE BOOKS and **2 FREE GIFTS** with no obligation to
purchase anything!

Visit us at:
www.ReaderService.com

YOUR OPINION POLL
THANK-YOU FREE GIFTS INCLUDE:

▶ **2 HARLEQUIN INTRIGUE® BOOKS**
▶ **2 LOVELY SURPRISE GIFTS**

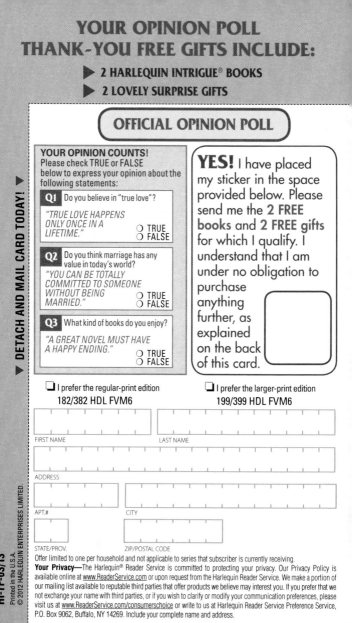

OFFICIAL OPINION POLL

YOUR OPINION COUNTS!
Please check TRUE or FALSE below to express your opinion about the following statements:

Q1 Do you believe in "true love"?

"TRUE LOVE HAPPENS ONLY ONCE IN A LIFETIME."
○ TRUE
○ FALSE

Q2 Do you think marriage has any value in today's world?

"YOU CAN BE TOTALLY COMMITTED TO SOMEONE WITHOUT BEING MARRIED."
○ TRUE
○ FALSE

Q3 What kind of books do you enjoy?

"A GREAT NOVEL MUST HAVE A HAPPY ENDING."
○ TRUE
○ FALSE

YES! I have placed my sticker in the space provided below. Please send me the **2 FREE books** and **2 FREE gifts** for which I qualify. I understand that I am under no obligation to purchase anything further, as explained on the back of this card.

◀ **DETACH AND MAIL CARD TODAY!** ▶

❏ I prefer the regular-print edition
182/382 HDL FVM6

❏ I prefer the larger-print edition
199/399 HDL FVM6

FIRST NAME

LAST NAME

ADDRESS

APT.#

CITY

STATE/PROV.

ZIP/POSTAL CODE

Offer limited to one per household and not applicable to series that subscriber is currently receiving.

Your Privacy—The Harlequin® Reader Service is committed to protecting your privacy. Our Privacy Policy is available online at www.ReaderService.com or upon request from the Harlequin Reader Service. We make a portion of our mailing list available to reputable third parties that offer products we believe may interest you. If you prefer that we not exchange your name with third parties, or if you wish to clarify or modify your communication preferences, please visit us at www.ReaderService.com/consumerchoice or write to us at Harlequin Reader Service Preference Service, P.O. Box 9062, Buffalo, NY 14269. Include your complete name and address.

HI-TF-03/13
Printed in the U.S.A.
© 2012 HARLEQUIN ENTERPRISES LIMITED

staying in control. It had worked that night. As blood had poured from him onto the sidewalk, he'd managed to stay conscious, to keep breathing, to hang on.

But when her sweet lips had touched his, he'd buckled. Caved. He'd screwed up.

Not that kissing her hadn't been wonderful. Her mouth had been hot and wet and she'd tasted like butterscotch candy. And damn, he'd always had a sweet tooth.

He shoved his half-eaten lunch away. Nightmare raised his head at the sudden noise. "Hey, I'm human," Sam explained to the dog. "It's not a crime to like kissing a pretty woman."

Nightmare stood up, turned around twice and then flopped on the floor, his butt in the air toward Sam, as if he knew that Sam had kissed other pretty women in the past and that none of them had made him want to howl at the moon.

Now what was he supposed to do? He'd kissed her, wanted badly to kiss her again, and knew if he did that he'd have earned lifetime membership in the dumber-than-dirt club.

He knew what he had to do. He picked up the phone and dialed before he could convince himself otherwise. Cruz answered on the fourth ring. "Hi, it's me," Sam said.

"I'm glad you called back. We never talked about the mailroom guy at Alexander and Pope," Cruz said.

He'd been so caught up in kissing Claire that he'd almost forgotten that Cruz had planned to go there yesterday. "What did he say?" Sam asked, willing to do business first.

"He has no recollection of any specific envelope that got delivered to Claire. Ms. Fontaine, as he referred to her. Every office in that building uses the same mailroom. It's a shared service offered by the landlord of the building. He said there are over four hundred people that he picks up mail from and delivers to. Does the route twice a day. People also bring mail directly to the mailroom, some of it is interoffice mail, some of it gets mailed out."

"He goes to four hundred different desks every day?"

"No. There's a mail bin near the front of every office where people drop off the outgoing mail. He sorts the incoming mail and delivers it to the receptionist and he doesn't know what happens to it after that. I suspect every department may do it a little differently. Some probably have mail slots."

He would need to ask Claire how mail got to her desk. "Okay, we can chase that down later today," he said. "I'm on my way in."

"Okay, I'll see you—"

"Hey, Cruz," Sam said, interrupting his friend. "I want you to take Claire out to dinner."

There was a long pause. Finally, Cruz spoke. "Sam, I think you may be low on oxygen. Try taking a few deep breaths."

"Don't be an idiot," Sam said. "Can I count on you?"

Cruz sighed. "Sam, I don't want to date. I can't do this."

"Please, I'm begging you. Take her out. Have a nice dinner. She needs this."

Cruz let out a louder, more deliberate sigh. "I swear I do not understand this. At all. But if it makes you happy and we can stop talking about this, I'll call her later."

Sam knew he was asking a lot from Cruz. The man was still in love with his ex-wife. But he didn't know what else to do.

Knowing that Claire was Tessa's little sister should have been enough to keep him from wanting her. A thousand things should have kept *her* from wanting him.

"Maybe you should call her now," Sam said. "That would probably be best."

He hung up the phone, turned and once again spied the brown paper sack. Knowing her and her propensity to find trouble, she'd probably get light-headed, slip on the stairs and crack her head open. As if he didn't have enough on his conscience. He picked up the sack and on his way out of the kitchen, put it on the entryway table, right next to his keys. It wouldn't kill him to drop off her lunch.

An hour later, when Sam arrived at work, Cruz was at his desk, his shirtsleeves rolled up and a phone to his ear. Sam almost turned around. If it was Claire on the other end, eavesdropping wasn't an alternative. There was only so much a man could take. He might have initiated the contact, but he didn't need to be present to hear it consummated.

But both Cruz's words and tone made it clear that it wasn't Claire. "Don't screw with me," his partner said, his tone menacing. Cruz had his head bent, scribbling on a yellow legal pad. A half-drank cup of coffee sat next to him. Sam tapped on the edge of the desk to get his attention.

Cruz looked up, nodded, then wrote something on the paper. He pushed it toward Sam.

Franco Capris. Formerly a dealer—guns, narcotics, hot merchandise of all kinds. Currently one of their best informants. Three years ago, Franco, or Frances as his mother had christened him just twenty-two years ago, had had a mature respect for what three years in prison might mean. He'd turned over quickly, made a deal and now generally his information was accurate. Right now, however, it didn't look like Cruz was buying it.

"You're sure?" Cruz questioned.

He listened for a long minute. "Okay," he finally said. "Keep in touch." He hung up and scratched his head.

"I decided it wouldn't hurt to describe the pawnshop

woman to Franco and it looks like I hit gold. He knows her. Not her name, but she runs a little business on the corner."

"Prostitution?"

Cruz shook his head. "Drugs."

"What kind of drugs?"

"Said he didn't know, but she has a lot of repeat customers."

"Was he being straight with you?"

"He has been in the past. He said he'd keep his ear to the ground." Cruz pointed to a piece of paper in the middle of Sam's desk. "The lab report came back on the letter Claire got. They couldn't get a print."

Sam sat down and read the brief document. "Damn," he said. "None of this makes any sense. First, Claire's apartment gets robbed. Maybe no big deal. Happens all the time in the city. But then, a month later, Sandy Bird, a stranger to both Claire and Nadine, breaks in with no apparent motive. And we find absolutely no connection between Sandy or her husband to either Claire or Nadine." He rubbed his forehead. His head hurt. "Then Claire gets the phone call. The caller knows more than he should about something that happened years ago. Then, most recently, Claire gets that piece of trash at work. Not exactly a threat but creepy enough to make her nervous. Who would want to do that? Why? We don't have any reason to believe the letter is related to Sandy Bird or the robbery, but if it is…"

Cruz waited for him to finish. When Sam didn't, Cruz said it for him. "It makes it seem as if Claire was the target all along."

Sam looked away, unable to meet his partner's eyes. "Yeah, that's exactly what it looks like, especially because it all started with her stuff getting stolen. Now it turns up, maybe pawned by a dealer who peddles high-quality. I think I might be losing my mind," he said, shaking his head.

"By the way, I talked to Claire about twenty minutes ago."

Cruz's tone had been casual, yet Sam could hear the underlying hint of something else. If he didn't know better, he might think it was nervousness. "Okay," Sam said, proud that his voice didn't crack.

"She said yes."

Well, wasn't that great? "So what's the plan?"

"Dinner and a movie. Tonight."

"Tonight?" The word exploded from his mouth, ruining his I'm-really-not-interested attitude. "I thought she was working late tonight."

"Evidently not." Cruz started to look a little irritated.

"But it's a weeknight," Sam said.

"Dinner and a movie," Cruz repeated, his tone hard. "She'll be home by eleven, *Dad*."

Sam could feel the heat rise and knew that his face was probably red. "Are you picking her up?"

Cruz slammed down his coffee cup. "Sam, you're a nut job. First, you tell me to ask her out and when I do, you make me feel like I screwed up. What's going on with you and Claire?"

It had sure seemed like there was something going on earlier. Going on, about to go off. It had been close.

And it had been a huge mistake—totally his fault. She'd been confused. It was his responsibility to keep things on the straight and narrow.

Sam shoved his desk drawer in so hard that the stack of papers on the edge of the desk started to slide. He grabbed for them and knocked his stapler onto the floor.

Cruz looked at him as if he'd lost his mind. Maybe he had. "That's it," Cruz said, picking up his phone. "I'm calling her now and telling her that this is a mistake. You need to—"

"Stop this," Sam finished the sentence. "Look, Cruz, I'm being an idiot. This is exactly what I want."

"You're sure?"

"Absolutely."

"Did I just hear you accept a date? A real I'll-pick-you-up-and-pay-your-way kind of deal?" Hannah leaned over the edge of the gray cubicle wall, her eyes heavy with mascara and wide with excitement.

Claire wished she could feel the same way. She should. It was her first date in Chicago. With a handsome guy. What was the problem?

It wasn't with Sam.

But Sam had suggested it. When Cruz had said that, Claire's hopes had crumbled. Sam wasn't interested. The message couldn't have been clearer. So she'd said yes to Cruz. Why not? What else could she do? She'd practically flung herself at Sam two hours ago. He'd been surprised but recovered nicely. It practically made her want to squirm in her chair to remember how nicely he'd recovered. It had been wonderful.

Then it had been like being dumped in a cold lake when he'd pulled away. She didn't think the chill had left her bones yet. No way could she spend the evening at Sam's, pretending that she wasn't hurting. A dinner and a movie really would be perfect.

"Where's he taking you for dinner?" Hannah asked.

Claire couldn't resist. "Paris. He's got a private jet."

"Oh, my God," Hannah squealed and Claire worried that the woman might actually throw herself over the cubicle wall. She could hear other chairs being pushed away from desks as coworkers developed an interest.

"I'm kidding," she hissed. "Dinner and movie. Here. In Chicago. I'll probably have to leave the tip."

Hannah's face fell. "Still," she said, "it's a date. What are you wearing?"

"Probably what I have on."

Hannah looked shocked. "You're going to wear a brown dress on a date?"

"Taupe, not brown."

"Even worse. I know the perfect thing. That little black dress you wore when we went to Bartolucci's for dinner."

"It was August and ninety degrees. I'll freeze in that."

"Wear a wrap over it. Something sexy."

Hannah wasn't going to give up. "Fine."

"I want a full report. Details."

"Fine," Claire said again. She studied the papers on her desk, hoping Hannah would get the hint. What the heck had happened? A few days ago, her life had been simple. Now, things cluttered it up—a dead woman on her couch, creepy notes, Sam's partner and finally, last but not least, Sam.

She'd be able to cross him off her list in a week or so. She needed to talk to Nadine. They'd do it together, the way they always had.

Chapter Ten

At fifteen minutes before three, Claire's intercom light buzzed. "Claire Fontaine," she answered, keeping her eyes on her computer.

"Claire, there's a Sam Vernelli here to see you. He wasn't on the schedule of today's visitors. I *told* him that our staff doesn't usually see people without an appointment."

Sam. His coming to her office couldn't be good news. "I'll be right out," Claire said, trying to quell the sudden panic. When she got to the reception area, he had his back to her, looking out the seventh-floor window. The fall sun was high in the almost-cloudless blue sky and the long reach of its rays caused the whitecaps of Lake Michigan to sparkle.

When she'd stood before that same window, she'd always felt tiny in comparison to the wide expanse of the lake, like an inconsequential piece of matter that could be swept away. But now she was struck by how Sam filled up the small space, not small at all. It wasn't just his physical size, although six feet of pure muscle was pretty hard to ignore, it was also his presence. His air of competence, his sense of purpose, his demeanor of calmness.

Then he turned around and she suddenly wasn't so sure that he was all that calm. He looked almost agitated.

"What happened?" she asked.

"Nothing," he rushed to assure her. "You, uh, forgot your linner, you know, lunch and dinner."

She'd realized that shortly after arriving at the office. It had been one more reason why Cruz's dinner invitation had sounded good. She stared purposefully at Sam's empty hands.

"I meant to bring it to you," Sam added, "but I forgot it on my desk. So I thought maybe you and I could go out and grab a bite."

Face-to-face, with only a small table between them. They'd knock knees and she'd spontaneously combust. "That's not necessary," she said. "I'm going out to dinner."

"I know. That's…uh…what I want to talk to you about."

"Why?"

"Claire," he said, clearly exasperated with her. He looked over toward the receptionist desk where Marcy was clearly listening to everything. "Can we please just go get something to drink? Is that too much to ask?"

He had no idea. "Fine," she said finally. "Let me get my purse." When she turned to go back to her desk, he fell in step next to her. "I'm not going to run out the back door," she said.

He shrugged. "I'm not worried about that. I'd like to see your work space. Is that where you put your outgoing mail?" he asked, pointing toward the office mail bin.

God, he was such a cop. "Yes."

"Does she get your incoming mail?" Sam asked, cocking his head in Marcy's direction.

"Yes. Sorts it and then puts it in the mail trays on our desks."

"I'll probably want to talk to her."

Marcy would *love* that. Heck, maybe Sam wouldn't find

it all that objectionable either. He didn't need to feel responsible for Marcy. And she was definitely closer to his age.

The whole idea of it infuriated Claire. "Maybe you'll
want to check my coworkers' desks, too," she suggested.
"Ask them to show you their black markers."

It was petty and mean-spirited, but that was pretty much
how she was feeling. But Sam seemed determined to ignore her sarcasm. He just shrugged.

Claire led him to her desk. She hoped Hannah was
somewhere else. But as luck would have it, the woman was
just rounding the corner of the cubicle wall.

"Claire?" Hannah inquired, staring at Sam.

"Uh, Sam, this is my friend, Hannah. We share a cubicle
wall. Hannah, this is Detective Sam Vernelli."

Hannah stared at Sam, her eyes narrowing. "My, my,"
she said. She looked at Claire and winked before extend-
ing a hand to Sam. "Lovely to meet you. Really. What's
going on?"

"Detective Vernelli and I are going to get something
to drink. In fact," Claire said, her brain finally starting to
function, "why don't you join us?"

A deep breath left Hannah's body, taking her from a size
twenty to an eighteen. "I don't think so. You two have fun,"
she said, as she squeezed past them. "Bye, now. Behave."
She waved her hand over her shoulder. The bangles on her
wrist clinked together and the fluorescent lighting caught
the sparkle of the four rings she wore on her plump fingers.

Sam looked a little stunned. "She's something," he said.

Yeah, well, Something had just deserted her to play
matchmaker. "We better go. I've got a lot to do."

Ten minutes later, she and Sam had a tiny table at a
crowded bistro. She'd ordered an iced tea and he ordered
a soda. The people at the table next to them both had some
kind of pasta dish. It made her remember how she'd made

him spaghetti. Earlier, when she'd gotten the jelly out of the refrigerator to make her sandwich, she'd seen the plastic container still there, untouched.

Sort of like her.

"Your office is nice," he said. "Great view."

"Uh-huh." The server brought their drinks and she kept herself busy squeezing lemon into her tea.

"Your receptionist may be part pit bull. I never considered showing up without an appointment to be a federal offense before."

That made her smile. She was still a little afraid of the woman. "That's Marcy. Her brother is my boss. I don't think she thinks it's necessary for her to be polite or to even work for that matter. Victor likes her up front because she's pretty, she dresses nice and she sure as heck knows how to screen a visitor."

"The intake officers at Cook County Jail are more welcoming. Anyway, where was Mission?"

She shrugged. "Maybe out on a client call. Look, Sam, you had something you wanted to tell me?" she asked, looking at her watch.

"I talked to Cruz this morning. He mentioned that you two are going out tonight."

"Yes."

Sam waited, like he expected her to say more. She took a drink of her tea.

"You know, he's had some rough times lately."

She swallowed. "Rough?"

"He and his wife split. They were married quite a while and really, the ink is barely dry on the divorce papers."

Now she was getting a headache. "Sam, I'm confused. Cruz said that you encouraged him to call."

"He told you that, huh?" Sam pulled on his tie like it had suddenly gotten too tight around his neck.

She nodded.

"I did. He's really a great guy. I love him like a brother. But I…like you, too."

Had he almost said love? Impossible. Hope flared, warming her. She put her hands in her lap, not wanting to take the chance that he'd see that her hand had started to shake.

"And," he continued, "I'm responsible for you. I'm the closest thing to family that you've got here and somebody needs to watch out for you."

Emotion surged through her as she heard what he left unsaid. *After all, he'd practically been her brother-in-law.* She wanted to push the table over and throw a few chairs through the plate-glass window. She was *always* going to be Tessa's little sister, somebody who needed to be taken care of, somebody who evidently wasn't smart enough to take care of herself. It was the second time in less than twenty-four hours that Sam had given her the responsibility speech and she was tired of it.

She shoved her chair back from the table and the wrought-iron legs made a screeching sound against the slate floor. "Here's a news flash, Sam. I'm not your responsibility. I don't need or want you to watch out for me. I can take care of myself. So butt out. Stick your nose in somebody else's business."

The people around them had stopped eating. Sam ignored them and stood up, reaching for her arm. "Claire, calm down," he said.

She yanked her arm away, sending a basket of rolls flying out of the hand of an unsuspecting waiter. The young man scrambled after the rolling pastry and the rest of the waitstaff stopped to look. "I am calm," she yelled. "And I know exactly what I'm doing. I'm wasting time. That stops now. What was it you said the other night? That girls my age need to experiment?"

None of the other customers even bothered to pretend they weren't listening. Sam's face lost all its color. "That was just—"

"Brilliant," Claire said. "Smartest thing you've said to me." She could feel the tears coming, but she would not cry in front of Sam again. She got four steps away from the table before she turned back. "Don't wait up, Sam. It'll be a late night."

SAM WRENCHED OPEN HIS car door and dropped down on the seat. He picked up the brown lunch sack next to him and tossed it from hand to hand until finally he squeezed his hands together, compressing the sandwich and grapes into one big ball of mush.

"Great idea," he said, throwing the soggy brown paper ball onto the floor. He'd had every intention of dropping off her lunch, hadn't even planned to see her. Then, at the last minute, he hadn't been able to walk away. He'd needed to warn her.

"About what, you idiot?" he asked, looking in the rearview mirror. He didn't look any different but he sure felt stupid. He'd gone nuts over dinner and a movie. What the hell was he going to do now that he'd practically pushed her into his friend's bed?

CLAIRE FELT A LITTLE foolish standing in the apartment, her breasts spilling over the bodice of her dress. It must have shrunk at the dry cleaners. Nightmare studied her. "I should change, shouldn't I?" Claire asked. Nightmare barked, a sharp yelp that Claire took for a yes.

Even the dog thought she looked ridiculous. After the

debacle at the restaurant, she'd barely been able to concentrate on the growing pile of work on her desk. She hoped that she never had the opportunity to eat in that restaurant again. Security camera tapes had no doubt been pulled and her picture plastered up by the entrance, right next to the "We reserve the right to refuse service to anyone" sign.

Hannah, of course, had been waiting at her desk when she'd returned, wanting to know everything. Claire had felt like slime doing it, but she'd looked the woman in the eye and lied. *Great time. Best tea in town.* Hannah had looked disappointed but hadn't pushed.

Claire took a step toward the bedroom, intent on changing into something with sleeves and a turtleneck collar, but stopped when the doorbell buzzed. She did not want Cruz cooling his heels while she changed her outfit. That seemed like something a girl did when she and the guy were already a couple.

Instead, she grabbed a sweater off the chair and pushed her arms into the sleeves. When she opened the door, Cruz stood there, holding a small bouquet of flowers in his hands.

"These are for you," he said, shoving them toward her. His voice had cracked.

"Thank you," she said, suddenly more relaxed. He was as nervous as she was. "I love daisies." She grabbed a glass out of the cupboard, filled it with water and stuck the flowers in it.

Cruz shuffled his feet. "They were Meg's, my ex-wife's, favorite, too."

"How long have you been divorced?" Claire asked, remembering Sam's comment about the wet ink.

"Six months, eleven days," Cruz said. He rolled his eyes and looked embarrassed. "Not that I'm counting."

Claire linked her arm in his and shut the door behind them. "Tell me all about her," she said as they walked down the hall.

WHERE THE HELL WERE THEY?

Sam paced around his kitchen, stopping every so often to take a swig of his beer and stare at the flowers. Cruz had brought her flowers? Good Lord.

He'd said that he'd have her home by eleven. It was almost thirty minutes after that. Sam picked up his cell and almost pressed Cruz's number before he managed to stop himself. He deserved this torment. He'd arranged this. Hell, if Claire found her way to Cruz's bed, Sam had nobody to blame but himself. He'd practically plumped up the pillows for them.

When he heard Claire's laugh outside the door, Sam dived for the couch, grabbed the remote and flipped on the television. The door opened and Claire came in.

"Hey, Sam," Cruz said, following close on Claire's heels. "What are you doing? Brushing up on your Spanish?"

It took Sam a moment to realize that Cruz was pointing at the television. Great. A Spanish soap opera. Sam flipped through the stations, killing time, hoping for breath. His lungs felt empty, like they might collapse at any moment.

Skin. Beautiful, honey-colored, bare skin. Claire's dress, he guessed some might call it that, hugged her in all the right places. Did she even have a bra on?

He just bet Cruz knew the answer to that one. And Cruz, who generally wore nothing but cargo shorts and old T-shirts on his off-time, had on dress slacks and a nice shirt. He even wore shoes instead of his customary sandals.

"You're late," Sam said, flipping off the television. "Extra-long movie?" he prodded.

Both Claire and Cruz looked blank. Ugly, dark suspicions crowded Sam's oxygen-deprived brain. "You *did* go to a movie?" Sam asked, forcing himself to stay seated.

"Actually, no," Cruz said, looking a little unsure.

Sam got up and circled around them, taking a position on Cruz's left. The man had been his best friend for five years. He trusted him. But Cruz was also wounded. Lonely. And Claire was a beautiful woman. "I thought that was the plan," Sam said.

Cruz held up a hand. "It's not what you—"

Claire turned toward Cruz. "Cruz, please. I don't think Sam needs the details."

Cruz looked from her to Sam. "Sam?" he questioned, clearly uncomfortable.

God, this was killing him. "She's right," he said. "It's none of my damn business."

Claire squeezed Cruz's hand and said, "I had a nice night."

"Yeah, me, too," Cruz said.

Sam flipped the remote control onto the couch and walked toward his bedroom door. "So everybody had a nice night. That's great. Just great."

Chapter Eleven

At five the alarm went off. It should have woken Sam up, but because he'd been awake for most of the night, burning up with some strange emotion that seemed an awful lot like jealousy, all it did was irritate the hell out of him.

Claire was already up. He'd heard the shower turn on about ten minutes ago.

He walked to the kitchen to start coffee, shaking his head at Nightmare who lay sprawled in front of the bathroom door. "You're pathetic," he said to the dog. He measured out the coffee, filled the canister with water and flipped the switch. When the hot liquid started to stream out, he opted to hold a cup under it. When it was almost full, he heard the bathroom door open and then Claire's door close right away. He shoved the coffeepot back into place.

If he hurried, he'd have time for a quick shower before she got dressed. Walking toward the bathroom, he took a gulp, burning his tongue and throat. When he opened the bathroom door, the room was warm and the mirror covered with steam. The room carried her scent, making him think of oranges and lemons. He took a deep breath and held it. Not once, but twice. Then, shaking his head, he shucked off his clothes and stepped into the shower.

And then he thought about how Claire had been standing in that same spot just minutes ago, naked. Like some sick fool, he ran his hands across the door where beaded up water clung to the glass. He rubbed his wet fingers together and pressed them up against his lips, imagining the water skimming the slope of her breast, then dripping off the tip of her nipple. He saw the water run across her flat stomach, into the vee of dark hair at the top of her legs.

Sam sank down on the floor, not caring that the hot water sprayed beyond him. He was way more pathetic than his dog. All Nightmare did was follow Claire around and wait for her. Sam took it to a new low, standing in the stupid shower, fantasizing about her. He should be shot.

He'd loved her sister.

Not that Claire reminded him much of Tessa. It wasn't just the physical differences, but more so the way she'd responded to everything. The dead woman in her apartment had shaken her. Sure. But she'd snapped quickly back, demonstrating a steadiness that he respected. Tessa had never had that quality. She'd vacillated from very happy to very sad, sometimes in the span of minutes.

There were other differences, too. Claire had obviously taken college seriously. Tessa had never been a good student and had been more interested in partying than studying. She'd thought nothing of staying up all night and sleeping past most of her classes the next day. They'd argued about it more than once. At the time, he'd been sure she'd outgrow it.

But she'd never had the chance. She'd had her life stripped away and the bastard who'd done it had walked away. And when she'd died, a part of Sam had died, too.

He shifted, feeling the heavy need of his body. And now, he was sitting here, hard as a rock, thinking about her sister.

Who he'd pushed into Cruz Montoya's arms. Maybe his bed. He'd practically begged the man.

Be careful what you ask for. His mother's eleventh commandment. Hell.

Ten minutes later, still chilled from what ended up being a very cold shower, Sam stood in the kitchen. He was halfway through a bowl of cereal when Claire walked in.

"Oh. I didn't expect to see you this morning," she said.

My God she was beautiful. Her skin looked fresh, she smelled delicious and he had the craziest urge to touch the narrow gold hoops that hung from her delicate ears. She wore a conservative blue suit with some kind of scarf that only women knew how to tie. She had a briefcase slung over one shoulder. She looked very businesslike, very professional. And he tried to focus on that and to forget he'd ever seen the black dress.

"Look, Claire, I'm sorry about last night. I was a jerk. It's just that I…" He couldn't tell her he was jealous. "I'm responsible for you."

The strap of her briefcase slipped off her shoulder and the soft leather hit the floor with a dull thud. "I thought I told you that I don't want to be your responsibility."

He hated hearing the hurt in her voice. "It is what it is, Claire. We can't change the circumstances."

"Actually, Sam, we can. And sometimes, it's the only thing to do. Trust me on this one."

His chest hurt. Really hurt. "What do you mean?"

"I'm going back to my place. It's time. It's past time," she added.

"No," he barked. He took a breath. "No," he said, softly this time. "You could still be in danger. We still don't know how everything is connected. Please give me a few more days."

She stared at her cereal bowl. "Okay," she said. "But I'm

calling Nadine today and asking her to come back. Once she's in town, I'm going to leave."

He nodded. It was for the best.

Claire ate her cereal and packed her lunch. She didn't speak again until she opened the door and threw a casual *bye* over her shoulder.

With Nightmare on his heels, he walked over to the window and lifted the edge of the heavy curtain. He stood there for two minutes, watching until she was out of sight.

Then, slowly, feeling like an old man, he lowered himself down on the couch. He felt empty. And more lonely than he had in some time.

Later, he didn't know if it was ten minutes or an hour, he straightened up. He couldn't sit here all day. Claire might argue the point, but he did have a responsibility. If not *for* her, then *to* her. His job was to track down every possible lead.

It was time for him to meet Claire's boss. But with pit bull Marcy on duty, he'd probably lose a hand if he tried.

He opened his wallet and pulled out a business card for Victor Santini. There'd been a stack of them yesterday on Marcy's desk. He picked up his cell phone, dialed and got lucky when Victor answered his own phone.

Sam explained why he was calling. As he anticipated, Victor flatly denied the possibility that anyone on his team might have singled out Claire. "Everyone likes her," Victor said. "They respect her talent."

"Is it possible that anyone is jealous of her talent?" Sam asked.

Victor laughed. "The only person jealous of Claire is Marcy and that's not because of her talent."

"What do you mean?" Sam asked.

"I…well…" Victor hesitated, as if just realizing that he'd said too much. "Let me put it this way, Detective. Marcy tells everybody that she's twenty-six when she's really thirty-six. She's not exactly aging gracefully."

At only twenty-four, Claire was a logical target. But if the note was linked to the call, how could Marcy know anything about Tessa?

"Where did your sister work before she started at Alexander and Pope?"

"She didn't. She was married to an attorney."

"What's his name?"

"I don't know why it matters, Detective, but it was Matthew Strong."

Sam didn't recognize the name. But in a city the size of Chicago, there were probably twenty-thousand attorneys. Maybe the guy had been in the state attorney's office when there was discussion about the case. But that was a long shot.

It was eleven years ago. The case had never made big headlines because it never got litigated.

Hard to go to trial when there was no defendant, nobody to blame.

"I have to get going," Victor said. "Trust me on this, Detective. Cryptic notes are not Marcy's style. If she's got something to say, she says it to your face."

Sam hung up and opened his laptop. With a few clicks, he'd signed on to his computer and found the website for Alexander and Pope. He shook his head in disgust. On the website, for every kook and crazy to see, they had pictures of their employees. He looked at Claire's picture. Her eyes were bright, her smile perfect. She was beautiful.

He ignored the pain in his stomach and proceeded to print off copies of all the other pictures. The only saving grace was that the employee's names were not listed under their photos. It offered Claire some anonymity.

He left his house and drove directly to Claire's apartment building. Once inside, he climbed the three flights of stairs and knocked on the apartment door across the hall from Claire's.

When Mrs. Peters answered, she had a rolling pin in her hand. She was wearing the same robe and slippers as the first day he'd seen her.

"Mrs. Peters, I'm Detective Sam Vernelli." He handed her a card. "I'm investigating the shooting that occurred across the hall and I was wondering if you'd look at a few pictures for me."

"I'm not letting you into my apartment," she said.

"That's fine, ma'am. We can do it right here." He pulled out the folder. "I would just appreciate it if you'd look at these pictures and tell me if you've ever seen any of these people in the building."

She sorted through the pictures once, then again. She barely gave Marcy's picture a glance. She did study one carefully. "I've seen this guy. The first time was shortly after the girls moved in and then a few times after that."

"You're sure?"

She raised her rolling pin. "Just because I'm old doesn't mean I'm stupid."

"Of course not," he said. "Thank you for your time." Back in his car, he drummed his fingers on the steering wheel.

Pete Mission.

In Claire's apartment? Claire had been convincing when she'd said there had been no visitors in the apartment. And on the trip to his parents, when he'd tried to warn Claire about Mission, she'd seemed truly oblivious to the fact that the guy might be interested.

It didn't make sense. And when things didn't add up, he needed to start asking questions. He started his car and twenty minutes later he beached his car in a no-parking zone. He was inside and up to the seventh floor within minutes.

"Can I help you?" Marcy looked up from the magazine she was reading.

Sam forced a smile. Last thing he needed was her tipping his hand to Mission. "I'd like to see Pete Mission."

"Oh." She narrowed her eyes. "Weren't you just here yesterday to see Claire Fontaine about what happened at her apartment?"

"Yes. And today I'm here to see Pete Mission."

She smiled for the first time and tilted her chin up. "I hope I'm on your list of people to question, Detective."

Her tone was suggestive. It made his head hurt. It was pretty clear that her brother hadn't tipped his hand, hadn't told her that he'd let it slip that she might have a reason to dislike Claire. Probably didn't want to incur the woman's wrath for an entire day. Sam figured her the type to get in a snit and take it out on everybody.

"If you have any information that could aid in a police investigation," he said, "I'd want to know that."

She leaned forward, giving him a glimpse of what she likely considered her best assets. "I didn't say I had information. But I am, shall we say, interested."

He shook his head. "I'll just wait here while you get Mr. Mission." He turned and after a few seconds, heard her pick up the phone.

Mission made him wait ten minutes. When he finally did poke his head through the reception-area door, he looked pale. "Detective?" he asked.

"Is there someplace we could talk privately?" Sam asked, aware that the receptionist was all ears.

"It's a really busy day," Mission said, holding up some papers in his hand.

"That's too bad. It's *really* important," Sam answered, his patience wearing thin.

Mission rolled his eyes. "Fine. Follow me." He led him to a large conference room and shut the door behind them. "What can I do for you, Detective?"

"I'm investigating a robbery and a murder that occurred at Claire Fontaine's apartment."

"Yes." Mission's voice stayed calm, almost uninterested, but Sam could see the fine line of sweat above the man's lip.

"I have reason to believe that you've been in Claire's apartment."

Mission shook his head. "I don't think so," he said.

"You don't remember?"

"I don't know," Mission said, his tone defensive. "Do you remember every place you go, Detective?" The man started to pace around the conference-room table. "You know what, Detective? I saw the way you practically threw Claire into your car the other night," Mission said, his upper lip raised in a sneer. "I think that you've got more than a professional interest here."

Sam jabbed his arm out and grabbed Mission's tie, jerking him forward, until the man's face was just inches from his own. "I don't care what you think. Start talking. We do this here or we do it down at the police station."

"I...I know someone in her building," Mission said, his face turning red.

"Define someone."

"Jeff Wadell. We went to high school together. He's the super."

Sam released his hold on Mission and took a step back. "Keep talking."

"So I know that I've been in Claire's building because

I've stopped by a couple times and had a few beers with Jeff."

Was it possible that Mrs. Peters was half-right? She'd seen Mission in the building but not necessarily in Claire's apartment. The woman seemed pretty sharp, but then again, eye witnesses were notoriously unreliable.

Sam leaned in close, getting in Mission's face. "Claire got a note at work and it wasn't nice. You have anything to do with that?"

Mission looked confused. "What are you talking about?"

Now Sam knew the man could have been lying, but he didn't think so. He backed away from Mission. "The next time you want to have a reunion with your old high school buddy, do it at your place. Stay out of Claire Fontaine's building."

On his way back to the office, he once again detoured to Claire's building, and this time, he spent fifteen minutes with Jeff Wadell. He left, feeling fairly confident that the super was dumb as a box of rocks but not guilty of much else. He had confirmed that he and Mission were old friends and that they'd had a beer together sometime within the past couple of months.

When he got back to the office, Cruz had his face buried in a file. Sam hesitated, aware that for the first time in five years, it was awkward between him and his partner. But Cruz had a right to know what was going on, especially now that he might have a personal interest in the situation.

"Cruz?" he said. "Got a minute?"

His partner nodded, his face showing no emotion.

Sam decided there was no use putting it off. "Hey, I acted like an idiot last night. You did exactly what I asked you to do and for the record, I'm glad you and Claire had a nice time."

Cruz cocked his head. "You're so full of crap, Vernelli. The woman has you in knots, doesn't she?"

He wanted to deny it but wasn't that good of a liar. "We're not talking about me," he said.

Cruz leaned forward. "Sit down. You're right about one thing. You're an idiot. Certifiable. Last night, Claire and I spent four hours at my apartment. Eating pizza," he added quickly. "Talking. Well, mostly me talking. Her listening."

Sam held up a hand. "It's none of my business."

"I don't understand what's going on between you and Claire," Cruz said. "You're pushing her at other men and when your name comes up in conversation, her eyes light up and she smiles, like you're a box of good chocolate."

"Good chocolate?" Sam echoed, his throat feeling tight.

"Versus Brussels sprouts," Cruz added sarcastically.

Sam dropped into a chair and faced his partner. "I don't know what the hell I'm doing. It's all crazy. I loved her sister."

Cruz nodded, looking serious. "I know you loved Tessa, but she's dead. She's been dead for a long time. You've got to move on, Sam. And while Claire might not be the easiest choice, sometimes we don't get easy. We get difficult. Painfully difficult."

"Like you and Meg?"

"Yeah, just like that. I bored Claire with the whole ugly story last night. She was a trooper—didn't let her eyes glaze over even once."

"You and Meg will work it out," Sam said.

Cruz shrugged, his eyes filled with pain. "Every day it seems a little less likely. But learn from my mistakes, okay? You've got something good here. Hang on to it. With everything you've got."

SAM OPENED HIS DOOR and saw Claire sitting on his couch, with Nightmare at her side. It hit him hard how nice it might be to come home at night, after a tough day, and have somebody there to unwind with.

Not just anybody. Claire.

He stumbled over the rug.

"Hi," she said.

"Hi." He felt off-balance, as if he'd tipped a few back. Maybe he was getting sick.

"I…" he said.

She held up a hand. "No, me first," she said, her voice soft.

He sat down in the chair across from her. Nightmare barely gave him a glance, just snuggled closer to Claire's leg.

Lucky dog.

"Okay," he said.

"I'm sorry about last night and this morning," she began. "I'm not proud that I deliberately let you think that something had gone on between Cruz and me. Nothing happened. I don't want you thinking poorly of your friend."

"I don't," Sam said.

She licked her lips. "Well, good."

"Cruz told me that he spent the night obsessing about his ex-wife."

"He's desperately in love with her."

Sam nodded. "I know. I was stupid to let my mind take a right turn into the gutter."

She smiled but it didn't reach her eyes. "I'm a little embarrassed. After all, I talk a big game about being a responsible adult and then I act pretty childish. I'm sorry."

"No," he said quickly. "Don't apologize. You're clearly the mature person in this room. You've handled everything that's happened to you in the last couple of weeks.

You've stayed calm, asked the right questions, followed directions. Never once complaining." He paused. "I think you're amazing."

Her beautiful brown eyes opened wide. "I never expected you to say that."

He rubbed his hand across his face. "There're a whole lot of things happening that I never expected."

The air in the room was charged with electricity. His own senses seemed heightened. The light was brighter than usual and the air was thick with the scent of the flowers that remained in the middle of the kitchen table.

She blinked twice. "Sometimes unexpected things are good."

He swallowed hard. "Sometimes."

She stood up. "Mature adults ask for the things they want, right?" Her voice was tentative.

He could feel his heart rate accelerate. "Yeah. They don't expect other people to guess."

"I'm asking, Sam." She held out her hand. "Will you kiss me?"

He felt the air swoosh out of his lungs, like he'd been sucker punched in the stomach. Sweet, holy, mother of God. She couldn't possibly know that he teetered between self-control and self-indulgence or that her lips could be that one small push that would send him reeling in the wrong direction. He was on a very narrow ledge.

He stayed in his chair. No room for touching on the ledge.

"Please," she pleaded.

What was it Cruz had said? *Hang on. With everything you've got.* He stood up and stepped close. Then he carefully leaned toward her, bent his head and brushed his lips across hers. He heard her quick catch of breath, felt her shiver.

And when she closed her eyes and parted her lips, it didn't matter how high the damn ledge was, or how hard the landing might be. It only mattered that he touch her.

He kissed her again. When she opened her mouth and welcomed his tongue, he was a lost man. It was everything.

It was not nearly enough.

When he finally pulled back, they were both breathless.

"Yikes," she said.

He bent forward, braced his hands on his thighs and focused on breathing. In through his mouth, out through his nose.

"Are you okay?" she asked.

He nodded and straightened up. Any minute his heart would catch up. "Great," he said, his voice cracking. He could see that her pretty brown eyes were dancing. "Are you laughing at me?" he asked.

"I love the way you kiss," she said. She reached out and stroked the pad of her thumb over his bottom lip. "I love the way you hold me," she continued. "Like I'm precious."

Oh, damn. He brushed a kiss across her forehead. "You are precious. Exquisite. Sexy as hell. And the fact that you don't know it makes it all the more so."

She leaned her sweet body into him and when her breasts brushed up against him, he couldn't hold back a groan.

"Stop that," he pleaded. "I'm only human."

She stopped, her big eyes fixed on him. Then, very deliberately, she reached down and stroked him, her finger inside the zipper flap of his dress pants.

He wrapped his hand around her wrist. "What are you doing?"

"Take me to bed," she whispered.

He'd never wanted anything more. "No." He swallowed hard. "Claire," he said, desperately hoping that if he started talking he'd figure out something right to say. Something that would make her understand. "It's not that—"

She pressed her lips against him and when she slipped her tongue in his mouth, he was toast. Deeper. Hotter. He broke away. "Are you sure?" he asked.

She nodded, looking very serious. "Are *you* sure?" she asked.

He didn't need to hide the truth any longer. "I've been thinking about taking you to my bed for days."

She cocked her head to the side, considering. "If I hadn't asked, would you have asked me?"

"No," he said.

She smiled and slipped her hand into his. She tugged him toward the bedroom. "Then I'm awfully glad I showed great maturity and asked for what I wanted. This is working out pretty well for me."

Chapter Twelve

She'd been so hot, so wet that Sam thought it was a miracle that he hadn't come on the first stroke. But by some crazy twist of fate, he'd been able to hold back, to make sure that she'd come first.

His orgasm had been mind-blowing and now he was spent. She lay next to him, on her side, one leg hooked over him, and he stroked her back with his free arm.

"Are you okay?" he asked.

"Wonderful."

He stretched, wondering what the hell kind of magic she had. He shouldn't even be able to move after what they'd shared and now he already wanted her again. He pulled her over his body so that she sat astride him.

"Me? On top?" she squeaked.

He guided himself in, loving the tight squeeze.

"Ooh." She closed her eyes and smiled.

Ooh. It echoed in his head. He lifted both of her heavy breasts and rubbed a thumb over each nipple. Then again. Her body shook in response. "You like that?" he whispered.

She nodded.

He pulled her forward until he could tug on one nipple with his mouth. He could feel the answering ripple in every one of her muscles. It was heat, it was power, it was perfect.

She was absolutely perfect.

CLAIRE WOKE UP lying on her side, her butt nestled against Sam's front. His arm was wrapped around her and his hand splayed across her abdomen. When she shifted, he pulled her tighter against him. "Good morning," he whispered in her ear.

"Good morning," she responded, not sure what else needed to be said. *Thank you* hardly seemed appropriate. *It was really swell* seemed a little cold. *Hope we can do it again,* a little presumptuous.

What she really wanted to do was turn in his arms, look into his eyes and tell him that she loved him. She'd known it before, but during the night, when they'd been as close as two people could be and they'd shared the secrets of their bodies, she'd been sure. She'd fallen in love with Sam Vernelli.

And what would she do if he didn't feel the same way about her?

Had it been love that had brought him to her bed or just lust? She wouldn't ask, wouldn't let him know how important the difference was to her.

"I'm hungry," she said, desperately wanting to think about something regular, something mundane.

"What time is it?" he asked, lifting his head. In the process, he kissed her bare shoulder and, if possible, she felt warmer.

"Almost six," she said. It was time to get up, otherwise they'd both be late to work. She didn't usually work on Saturday, but it hadn't been a usual week and even when she was there, she hadn't been as productive as she could or should have been. When she'd told Sam in the middle of the night that she intended to work the next day, he'd sighed loudly and then admitted that he intended to work, as well.

They would both probably fall asleep at their desks by mid-afternoon. Not much sleeping had gotten done last night. They'd made love three times and each time had been more perfect than the time before. But now, reality could not be ignored.

Sam sat up in bed and she was once again stunned at the sheer beauty, the sheer masculine perfection, of his body. Broad shoulders, muscular arms, flat stomach. She was glad the sheet covered the rest. She couldn't be held responsible when faced with such temptation.

"How hungry are you?" he asked, his eyes on her breasts.

She shrugged. "I could maybe wait fifteen minutes."

He pushed her back onto the starched white sheets and covered her body with his. "Fifteen minutes," he growled. "I need more time than that."

"I suppose," she said, arching when his fingers found her. "That I could always nibble on you."

The color drained out of his face.

And later when she nibbled and licked and did all kinds of delicious things to his body, she forgot about being hungry. She simply thought about the pure joy and splendor of being held in Sam Vernelli's arms and the pure power of seeing him fall to pieces.

CLAIRE WAS HALFWAY through her omelet when she flipped a page of the paper and saw the article. Chicago Cop Dies. She skimmed the story, her eyes moving fast.

It was horrible. A cop had made a routine traffic stop. He'd approached the vehicle and the suspect had shot him. He'd died at the scene.

The suspect had been caught just blocks away, but what

comfort was that to the dead man's family? He was survived by a wife and two children.

Claire picked up her coffee, but her hand was shaking and some of it spilled and spread across the newspaper. Sam could be taken from her. Cops responded to all kinds of crises every day. One minute they were walking, talking, having a bagel and a cup of coffee. The next, they were chasing bad guys.

Serving the people. Protecting them.

And never coming back.

Who protected the police officer? Who would protect Sam?

"Sam," she said, her voice quiet.

"Yeah?" he said, setting his own coffee down. He was reading the comics.

"I just want you to know," she said, "that last night was wonderful."

He smiled at her. "I already cooked you breakfast."

"I mean it," she said, impatient with his teasing. He needed to understand. "I want you to know that you made me happy. Happier than I may have ever been," she admitted.

He studied her, no longer smiling. "What was it like?" he asked, finally. "What was it like after Tessa died?"

She thought it might be the first time she'd heard him say Tessa's name that it hadn't seemed to be wrenched out of his soul.

That had to mean something, didn't it?

"Quiet. Very lonely," she said.

"How so?"

She shrugged. "I think losing a child is the worst thing that can happen to a parent. They felt like failures because they hadn't been able to protect Tessa. That's what parents are supposed to do—they're supposed to love and protect their children."

"So they focused on protecting you?"

"Almost to the point of wrapping me in cotton."

"What about the loving?"

He was good at spotting missing information. "I think they were afraid to love me," she said. "Because if they loved me that much and something happened, they knew they couldn't stand it. It would be more than they could bear. So they settled for protecting me."

He reached for her hand. His skin was warm and she could feel calluses on his palm. "I'm so sorry, Claire," he said.

"I was angry for a long time. Angry at them. Even angry at Tessa." She looked him in the eye. He needed to know it all. "When I was with my friends, I called her Saint Tessa. Because she was so wonderful, you know. She must have been to be loved so much."

She stopped, unable to go on. He must be disgusted with her.

He rubbed the pad of his thumb across the top of her hand. "You were so young," he said. "Too young to process it all. You were wallowing in your own grief—grief for a life that changed when she died."

She could feel the tears stinging the back of her eyes. "I stopped hating her at some point. Then I became obsessed with avenging her death. That's why I came to see you that night. I'm sorry. I made it seem like it was all about you, but really it was all about me. I'd spent years being jealous of a dead woman."

"Oh, honey," he said. He moved quickly. He squatted next to her chair and wrapped his big, strong arms around her.

She pressed her face into his shirt. "You don't think I'm horrible?"

"I already told you. I think you're amazing."

She lifted her face up. He kissed the tip of her nose.

When the doorbell rang neither one of them moved. It rang again and Sam stood up. "If it's someone selling something, I'm going to shoot them."

He went to the door and pulled back the shade.

Oh, holy hell. Lucille and Gregory Fontaine, Claire's parents, stood on his porch.

He hadn't seen them for eleven years but he'd have recognized them anywhere. They carried the same general air of disdain that he remembered, the same austere look.

He didn't want to open the door. It was funny, really. He faced bad guys every day, but he didn't know if he had the strength to do this. None of the bad guys made him feel like a gawky twenty-one-year-old kid again whose heart had been ripped out.

He opened the door. They stared at him. "Mrs. Fontaine. Mr. Fontaine," he said, his lips feeling stiff.

"Hello, Sam." Lucille Fontaine offered a brief smile. "You're looking well."

The woman he remembered had always had impeccable manners, too. Just one day after they'd laid Tessa's coffin in the cold ground, Lucille Fontaine had been at her desk, writing thank-you notes. He'd barely been able to lift his head up and she'd been taking care of social niceties.

"I've recently learned that we owe you a great deal of gratitude," she added.

"Yes, thank you for taking care of Claire, Sam," Gregory Fontaine said.

What was it Claire had yelled before rolls had started flying in the bistro? That she didn't need or want anybody taking care of her ever again. "I didn't do all that much, sir. Claire's pretty good at taking care of herself."

"Yes, well, that may be open for debate. We're grateful all the same," Gregory said.

If he knew Sam had had his daughter naked last night, he might not be so appreciative. He heard a noise behind him and turned to see Claire. Her face was pale.

"Hello, Claire," Lucille said. She didn't reach for her daughter. Gregory looked somewhere over Claire's shoulder and nodded.

Claire stepped forward and gave each parent a quick, awkward hug. Then she stepped back, close to Sam. "What are you doing here?" she asked.

"We saw Nadine at a church dinner with her parents." Lucille's tone, while still pleasant, held the undertone of censure. "I overheard her saying something to her mother. When I questioned her, she reluctantly told us everything."

"I didn't want to worry you," Claire apologized. "I'm sorry. But I'm fine. Truly. Everything is fine."

Her father, his face turning red, said a couple words not normally used in polite conversation.

Lucille looked a little embarrassed but didn't look like she disagreed. "You had a dead woman in your apartment, Claire. Everything is *not* fine."

Her father pulled what looked like airline tickets out of the inside pocket of his six-hundred-dollar suit. "We have less than an hour to catch our plane." The man handed Claire one of the tickets. Sam leaned over to read it. It was a ticket for travel from Chicago to Omaha, Nebraska, and it was made out in Claire's name. A one-way ticket.

Claire had said that they had settled for protecting her. What the hell would she do? Would she go?

Claire could still be in danger. The note gnawed at him. Who was the sick bastard who had written that?

The thief? If Sandy Bird hadn't been the thief, then

someone still walked the streets, someone who wanted to scare Claire for sure, maybe even hurt her.

Sam would die first.

And take the bastard with him.

"You're not safe here," Lucille said. "For God's sake, Claire, you could have been killed."

Like Tessa. The unsaid words hung in the air.

Claire's whole body shook and without thinking, Sam wrapped an arm around her.

"I'm sorry you found out from Nadine," Claire said. She sounded truly miserable. "I wanted to call you. I really did. I should have. I just knew you'd be so worried."

"We can talk about that when we get home," Gregory Fontaine said, looking at his watch. "I have a board meeting on Monday that I can't miss."

Claire held out the ticket and Sam could see the fine tremor in her hand. "Father." She stopped. When she spoke again, her voice was gentler. "Dad, I'm not going. I'm sorry. I won't do it."

Her father's head jerked up and her mother made a sound like she'd been sucker punched in the stomach. Sam remembered what Claire had told him the night he'd thrown her in the car at Pete Mission's house. Something about just recently beginning to say no and not always doing what she was told.

No wonder it had been so hard if that was the kind of reaction she got every time she dared to disagree.

Lucille Fontaine stepped forward. "Claire, how can you do this to us? How can you make us go through this again?"

"Don't be ridiculous," her father added, his tone harsh. "We're not here to discuss it. You're getting on that plane. We told you we didn't want you coming to Chicago, but you wouldn't listen to reason. It didn't even matter that we weren't going to provide any financial support. You had your mind made up. Well, now, I've got my mind made up. Get in the car, Claire."

Didn't they remember that she was up for the design award? They couldn't expect her to leave before that. Was it possible that she hadn't told them? Or did they just not care? Sam tried to quickly sort it out, but none of it made any sense. All he knew was that it felt way wrong.

He felt Claire take a deep breath. "But—" she began.

"How can you be so selfish?" Gregory Fontaine interrupted his daughter.

That did it.

"Actually," Sam said, looking her father right in the eye. "It's not Claire being selfish. It's me. You see, we're engaged. And I don't want my fiancée in Nebraska."

Chapter Thirteen

"Engaged?"

Claire had never heard her father use quite that tone of voice. It sounded like it came all the way from his toes.

Sam moved quickly, ushering everyone from the foyer to the living room. He pointed them toward chairs. Claire thought her mother looked like she needed one—she was the same color as the classic beige linen suit she wore.

What the heck had Sam been thinking?

Engaged? Oh, for goodness' sake, now what were they going to say?

She realized, very quickly, that she wasn't going to have to say much. Sam intended to do the talking.

"I know it's a bit of a surprise," he said, "but I hope you'll be as happy about the news as we are."

"Sam," her mother said as she sat down and fanned her face with her hand. "You can't be serious."

"It's crazy," her father said. "It's…it's sick, that's what it is."

"Sick?" Sam repeated, his tone still pleasant, but Claire could see the anger build in his eyes.

"Father," she said, "I know you didn't mean that."

"Be quiet, Claire. I did mean it. For God's sake, Sam. You were engaged to Claire's sister, too. If that's not sick, I don't know what is."

This had gone far enough. She knew what had prompted Sam's rash statement. Sam, who wanted to handle everything, had seen that her parents were about to bully her back to Nebraska. He'd decided to throw them a curve they couldn't have begun to anticipate.

Heck, she wished he'd warned her that he was about to pitch. She felt like she was still whirling, the momentum of her bat swinging her around, making her dizzy.

Wouldn't it be great if it were real? It'd be the home run of the century. A grand slam in the bottom of the ninth in the seventh game of the World Series. *Cubs Win! Cubs Win!* She could see the marquee now.

There it went, changing.

Sam and Claire! Engaged! Sam and Claire! The lights flashed and the crowd cheered.

She needed to stop this. Now. The Cubs weren't going to win the World Series and she and Sam Vernelli were not getting married.

"Sam, we need to tell—"

"—them the date," he finished. "Of course. January," he said with a smile. "Right after the holidays. You can imagine," he continued, "that we've got lots of planning to do. Claire can't possibly be in Nebraska."

"This is so unexpected," her mother said, her voice weak.

Tell me about it. Claire reached for her mother's hand and realized it was the first time in a very long time that she'd touched her mother, other than to offer an obligatory hug. When had her skin gotten so thin, like that of an old person's?

"Claire," her mother said, "are you sure?"

She nodded, afraid to speak.

Her father shook his head, looking disgusted. "We're going to miss our flight if we don't leave now."

"I'm staying," she said, finally finding her voice. "Here. With Sam."

Her parents looked at each other, then at both her and Sam. Sam didn't flinch, but he kept one hand cupped around her elbow, like he was prepared to hang on in the event her parents tried to strip her away.

Her mother looked like she wanted to cry. Instead, she stood, her back straight, her chin out. "I really don't know what to say."

Me either. "I'll call you," Claire said. "In a week or two. We can talk about this." That would be such a fun conversation.

Her father grabbed his wife's arm. "Let's go, Lucille," he said, pulling her after him. "We're not needed here."

As her parents walked away, Claire, feeling like they'd sucked up all her energy, took the chair her mother had vacated. Sam, looking a little sheepish, sat across from her.

"I guess I got a little carried away," he said.

A little? "Yeah, I guess. What was in your coffee?"

"You didn't want to go with them, did you?" he asked. He rubbed his index finger against the leather chair.

"Of course not," she said. "I wasn't going to."

"I just thought having a good reason to stay would help."

"There's just one thing. What happens when there's no wedding?"

He shrugged. "No problem. Whenever you're ready, you can tell them you wised up and dumped me."

It was the nicest thing anyone had ever done for her. "Sam, you don't have to do this."

"It's done, Claire. We're engaged."

Her heart jumped. If it were only true. If she thought for one minute that Sam Vernelli was madly in love with her, that he truly wanted to marry her, they'd be catching the next plane for Vegas.

He picked up his cell phone from the coffee table. "I need to call my parents."

Her heart felt heavy in her chest. "There's no need to tell them."

"Yes, there is. I wouldn't put it past your parents to call mine. I sure as hell don't want them hearing it that way."

"Then tell them the truth."

He shook his head. "That puts them in the position of having to lie. We sing the same song for the next month to everybody. No exceptions. Then there's absolutely no way to get tripped up. If we tell even one person the truth, then we've lost control of the situation."

"What are they going to think? What will Jake and Joanna think?"

He blinked a couple times. "I have no idea. It doesn't matter. What will Nadine think?"

Oh, man. How was she going to be able to keep Nadine from guessing the truth? She'd have to. She couldn't tell her the truth. Not after Nadine's most recent slip-up.

She had to admit that it hurt that Nadine hadn't been more careful. When she'd called her friend, she'd told her that she hadn't yet had a chance to tell her parents.

Still, she understood how relentless her parents could be. They'd sniffed the hint of a story and Nadine had probably had very little choice but to cough it up quickly.

"Mom, it's Sam. I've got you on speaker-phone. Claire's here with me."

"Hello, Claire. How are you, dear?"

"Well, thank you," she said. *Hang up,* she mouthed. This was a horrible idea.

Sam shook his head. He held up his index finger. *One month,* he mouthed back. "Mom, I…uh…wanted you and Dad to know that Claire and I are engaged."

There was a long moment of silence.

"Mom?"

"That's wonderful, Sam. Really. Congratulations. To both of you."

Claire could hear the unasked questions in his mother's tone.

"Let me get your father," she said.

There was at least two minutes of silence during which Sam's face was so stern that it looked like it was made of granite. She should not let him do this. She reached out and grabbed his wrist. His skin felt hot and it reminded her of when he'd pressed his hot naked body up against her. She let her hand drop. "It's not too late, Sam," she whispered. "Tell them it's a joke, tell them you had too much to drink last night and you're still hungover. Tell them—"

"Sam," his father came back on the line. His voice sounded steady. "I understand congratulations are in order."

"Thank you, Dad," Sam said.

"Have you talked to your brother?"

Sam swallowed. "Not yet. Maybe tomorrow. Claire and I have a lot to talk about yet. If you want, call him and tell him the news."

"All right, son. We love you."

"I love you, too," Sam said and hung up the phone.

He was pale and there was sweat on his forehead.

"My father was right," Claire said. She felt sick. What had they done? "This *is* ridiculous."

He didn't answer. He walked over, filled Nightmare's water dish and then pulled the shades up on both of the windows. It was a crisp fall day. "We need to get to work."

Her cell phone rang before she could answer. Not wanting to go another round with her parents, she checked the caller ID first. It was Nadine's cell phone.

"Hello."

"Oh, my God, Claire. I wanted to call last night but I fell asleep. Is everything okay?"

Okay? That sort of depended on one's definition of okay. She was with Sam, at his house. They'd spent the previous night making love. That should have meant everything was perfect. And it would have been if the engagement had been for real. "Sure. Everything's fine."

"But…" Nadine's voice trailed off. "Where are you?" she asked.

"I'm at Sam's."

Silence. "Have you talked to your parents?" Nadine asked, her tone cautious.

"Yes. They just left. It was a rather short reunion." It sounded so simple. How could it be so complicated?

"But you're not going back?"

"No."

Claire could hear Nadine suck in a breath. "That's great, Claire. Really. I thought I'd blown it for you when I saw your parents at the church dinner. They heard me say something to my mother and when they asked, I couldn't lie to them. My mom was standing right there. I just couldn't do it."

"It's okay. They had to know sometime."

"You're not mad?"

She had been. Sort of. But Nadine had been her friend for over fifteen years. Friendships like that weren't tossed away. Not because somebody made a mistake. "I just want to know what you were doing at a *church* dinner?" Claire asked, teasing her friend.

"My mother wanted me to go with her."

"Next time, do me a favor—*whisper*. That's kind of the general expectation in a church."

Nadine laughed, although Claire thought it seemed a

little forced. Of course her friend felt bad. Claire would just have to make sure she realized that she didn't hold it against her.

"When are you coming back to Chicago?" Claire asked.

"Today. I'll be there by late afternoon."

She needed to tell her friend about the engagement. The quasi-engagement. She didn't intend to do it in front of Sam. "I'll come by around seven, then. I need to talk to you about something."

"What? Don't keep me in suspense."

She looked at Sam. He was pretending not to be interested, but she knew him well enough by now to see the slight difference in his shoulders, the almost-imperceptible cock of his head.

"Have to. Got to go to work now." Claire disconnected the call and laid down her cell phone.

"Sounds as if you're still planning on moving in with Nadine. I thought maybe things might be different now," he said. He stuck his chin out. "We *are* engaged."

Except that they really weren't. But she wasn't ready to say goodbye yet. "Once I talk with Nadine, I'll be back. I'll stay the night. But Nadine's counting on me to cover my share of the rent."

"I could pay your rent," he said. "I—"

"No," she interrupted him. "I don't need anybody to pay my rent. I can take care of myself."

He rubbed his thumb and index finger together. "I never said you couldn't."

He sounded hurt. How could she blame him? He'd done this incredibly nice thing. He'd lied to his family. For her. Just for her. And she was acting like an ungrateful shrew.

She walked over and wrapped her arms around him. "Sam, I'm sorry. I know you were just trying to help."

"I want to make love to you," he said.

It was the first thing he'd said in the last two hours that wasn't crazy. "Tonight," she said, before she brushed her lips across his.

He had a month. His instincts had bought him that.

He'd always had good instincts.

Instinct had saved his life before.

Instinct had found a way to keep her parents at bay.

Not that Claire hadn't almost blown it. As soon as the words were out of his mouth, he'd felt her gather up her courage and he'd known that he had just seconds to shut her up and to convince her parents that it was true. It was some of the fastest talking he'd ever done.

Now he needed to tell Cruz, who was helping one of his younger sisters move into a new apartment. Sam dialed his friend's cell. "How's the move going?"

"She has too many shoes and apparently doesn't understand how to pack glassware so that it doesn't break," Cruz said with a hint of humor in his voice. Sam could hear his sister telling him to shut up in the background.

The Montoya clan was tight-knit. Cruz was the oldest and had practically raised his younger siblings.

"What time will you be done?"

"Couple hours."

"Okay, can you meet me at the little diner on Houston? The one that serves breakfast all day."

"Got a jones for some biscuits and gravy?"

"My arteries *are* feeling a little clean," Sam said. "Just meet me there, okay?"

Cruz sighed. "Fine. Noon. Order the coffee if you beat me."

Sam beat his friend by two minutes. He ordered two coffees and two orange juices, thinking Cruz could probably use the vitamin C.

"What's up?" Cruz said, sliding into the worn vinyl booth. He looked at the orange juice, ignored it and picked up his coffee cup. He took a deep drink. "How's Claire?"

"Fine." Sam tossed an unopened creamer from one hand to the other. Again. And again. "We're engaged," he said finally.

Cruz nodded. "Fancy that."

The waitress picked that moment to stop at the table. Sam stuck with just coffee and Cruz ordered a Danish.

"Fancy that?" Sam repeated, when the woman had walked away. "I said engaged, Cruz."

"Congratulations. She's a great girl."

Sam set down his coffee cup. "That's it? Congratulations? You don't think I'm crazy? I was almost married to her sister."

"That was a long time ago."

Sam rubbed his forehead. "That maybe doesn't make it right."

Cruz set down his coffee cup, too. "Sam, are you trying to talk yourself out of it?"

He didn't know what he was trying to do. All he knew was what had been a crazy impulse seemed less crazy as each minute passed. Now, he was almost to the point of thinking that he was almost sane.

Why the hell couldn't he marry her?

"She's almost nine years younger than I am," he said.

Cruz nodded. "She seems pretty mature for her age."

The waitress came and set down the food. Cruz spread a liberal amount of butter on his roll.

"Her parents think it's sick."

Cruz took a bite, chewed and swallowed. "You'll win them over."

He wanted to tell his partner the truth, but he'd made Claire promise that everybody would hear the same story.

"I don't know what the hell I'm going to do," Sam said, just as his cell phone buzzed. He pulled it off his belt. "It's my brother," he said. "Hey, Jake," he answered.

"Can you meet me?"

It was the same question he'd asked Cruz earlier. "Where are you?"

"At your house."

Sam could feel his chest tighten. "Is it Mom? Dad?"

"No, you idiot. It's you. Get your ass home. Now."

Sam heard the phone disconnect. Cruz looked at him, his eyes filled with laughter. "Sorry," he said. "Couldn't help but overhear some of that. I always knew I liked your brother."

Sam pulled some money out of his pocket and shoved it toward Cruz. "Here. I'll see you later."

It took him ten minutes to get home. Jake sat on the front steps, drinking a cup of coffee and eating a doughnut. "You give cops a bad name," Sam said, hugging his brother.

"Sit down, Sam," Jake said, scooting over on the cement.

"Where's Joanna and Maggie?"

"Home. Probably cuddled up on the couch."

Sam fought a smile. His brother had actually said the word *cuddled*. "So what brings you to Chicago, Jake?"

His brother lifted his face to the sky. "I don't know. Nice fall day. Warm sunshine. Lots of pretty leaves on the trees." He shifted and looked at Sam. "Oh, yeah. I hear you're getting married."

His parents must have called Jake immediately after hanging up with Sam. Jake must have been on the road in minutes. Sam couldn't tell anything by his brother's expression. Couldn't tell if he thought it was a great idea or if it was the most absurd thing he'd heard lately. Sam hated that because what Jake thought mattered.

"She's a beautiful woman," Sam said.

Jake nodded. "That's always a plus."

"She works out. She likes baseball. She even likes Nightmare." Sam held up fingers, ticking off Claire's attributes.

"Very helpful," Jake said.

"Good work ethic. Easy to talk to."

More nods from Jake.

"You don't look convinced," Sam said.

Jake pulled back. "I didn't know I had to be convinced. But if that's the case, I guess I'm not hearing anything that makes me think she's special."

Sam stood up. "She's special. She's got more special in her little finger than most people do in their whole body." He waved his hand, dismissing Jake. "You don't know what you're talking about." How could his brother be so damn dense?

Jake smiled and patted the step. "Sit down, Sam."

Sam stared at him. Then he sat down hard, the concrete jarring his tailbone. He put his head in his hands. "I'm so far gone I couldn't even tell you were yanking my chain."

"Don't worry," Jake said kindly. "The ability to think and reason comes back in time. If it's any consolation, it affects women the same way. Or so Joanna told me. Well, after the fact," he added drily.

Did Claire feel the same way? Like she couldn't catch her breath, like she couldn't remember what it was like before they were together. Did she feel dizzy and hot and kind of sick to her stomach?

Was she scared?

Jake stood up and wadded up the plastic paper that had been around his doughnut. He stuffed the garbage into his now-empty coffee cup. "I've got to go. I don't like being this far away from Joanna and Maggie."

"You drove two hundred miles to sit on my steps for five minutes?"

"I drove two hundred miles to make sure."

"Make sure of what?"

"Just to make sure. Take care, Sam. Give Maggie's almost Aunt Claire a hug for us."

Chapter Fourteen

When Claire arrived at her old apartment Saturday night, Nadine was already there, unpacking groceries. The place smelled like new paint and there was an empty spot where the couch had sat. The warm October wind blew through the open windows, causing the pale green curtains to flutter.

Claire dropped her purse on the table. Then she hugged her friend. "I missed you," she said.

"Same here, roomie," Nadine said. She was eating an apple. "I stopped to get us some fresh food. Thanks for cleaning out the fridge."

Claire spied a bag of chips on the counter and a jar of salsa. There was an open bottle of red wine and Nadine had already poured a glass. Claire opened the cupboard and got another glass. She poured her own wine and took a sip.

It felt good to get away from the office. Getting that note had changed everything. Every time she interacted with someone, she walked away thinking, *Is it you? Do you not like me?*

And on top of that, the incessant chatter about the awards dinner was getting on her nerves. She wondered if it was affecting Pete Mission the same way. He'd been short-tempered and didn't look as if he'd been sleeping well. She'd worked up the nerve to ask him what was wrong and he'd practically bitten her head off. *Nothing was wrong. He was just busy.*

Well, okay. She'd gotten the message and gotten the heck out of his space. She thought it was truly possible that he might win the design contest—he was very talented. She hoped so because maybe that would be enough to change his mood.

"Rough day?" Nadine asked.

"Does it show?"

"Maybe a little."

Claire wasn't surprised. Nadine had been her best friend forever. They'd seen each other happy and sad and every emotion in between. That's what made it so difficult to lie to her. But she was going to. Sam had been insistent. Nobody gets the truth.

"There's something you need to know," Claire said. She drummed her nails on the counter. "Sam asked me to marry him."

Nadine dropped her apple. It rolled across the floor until it hit the wall. "And you said yes?"

"I did."

Nadine opened her mouth, closed it, then opened it again. "You don't think it's just a little creepy that he was engaged to your sister, too?"

"That was eleven years ago, Nadine."

"Yeah, but are you ever really going to know when he's with you if he wouldn't rather be with her?"

"She's dead, Nadine." She could hear the flatness in her own voice. "He can't be with her."

Nadine chewed on her thumbnail. "I'm sorry, Claire. You just surprised me. Congratulations. When's the big day?"

"Sometime in January. We haven't picked a date yet."

"Do your parents know?"

"We told them this morning. They took it about as well as could be expected."

"So…" Nadine looked around the apartment. "I guess that means I need to find a new roommate?"

"Not right away," Claire assured her. If she wasn't careful she wasn't going to have any place to live. A month from now she could wind up with nothing. No Sam, no apartment, nothing but a big cardboard box to keep her warm at night. "I'm going back to Sam's tonight. I have to do some shopping tomorrow for this event I have Monday night, but I'll move back in Tuesday. I promise. The wedding isn't for months. You and I'll have lots more time together."

"What event?" Nadine asked, ignoring the rest of Claire's comments.

"The Chicago Advertising Association's Design-of-the-Year contest. I'm a finalist. I guess I forgot to tell you."

Nadine shook her head. "Wow. You've really got the magic touch, don't you? Everything always works out for you."

Claire shrugged, unsure of what to say. Nadine's tone was odd but then again, she'd probably surprised the heck out of her with the marriage announcement, so no wonder things seemed a little off. "It's a nice honor," she said.

"Is there a prize?"

"The winner gets fifteen thousand dollars."

Nadine raised her wineglass. "Here's hoping you win."

She took a cab from the apartment to Sam's house. She would normally have walked it, but Sam had called her this afternoon and said he'd pick her up. She'd argued that was unnecessary. He'd relented and asked if she would at least take a cab. She'd agreed.

If he asked her to stand on her head in the corner, she'd probably give it the old college try.

"Hi," she said. She smiled at Sam, who was standing in the hallway. His hair looked as if he'd been running his fingers through it. She bent down and patted Nightmare. "Hi, sweetheart."

"I get a regular hi and he gets a *hi, sweetheart*. This is so unfair."

She kissed him. Soundly. When she pulled back, she tilted her head. "Still think you're behind?"

He shrugged. "I'm okay with how the game is going." He paused. "So you told Nadine about us?"

"I did. She was a little surprised. She'll probably be less surprised in a month when I tell her we've called it off."

He took a step back, almost stumbling over the dog.

"Sam, what's wrong?"

"Nothing," he said.

She didn't believe that. He looked upset. "Did something happen at work today? Do you know something that you aren't telling me?"

He shook his head. "I've been thinking," he said. "You and I like a lot of the same things. Sports. Spaghetti. Dogs."

He was acting so odd. "What are you saying, Sam?"

He yanked at his tie, loosening it. "What I'm saying is that maybe we really should get married. After all, we're pretty compatible."

Compatible?

People who were compatible carpooled. They didn't get married. Her parents were compatible. Yuck. "Sam," she said, her heart feeling heavy, "that's not enough."

He took a step forward, she took one back until his big body crowded her up against the door. "We're good in bed," he said, his tone challenging.

She couldn't argue that. And when he put his hands

under her sweater, she didn't want to. And when he bent his head and kissed her, she thought he might be determined to convince her just how good compatible could be.

She'd be an easy mark. Like the car buyer who convinced herself that she couldn't live without a particular make or model all before the salesman ever stuck his head out the showroom door. "I'm hungry," she said.

He frowned at her. "Really?" he asked.

She nodded.

He grabbed his keys and billfold off the hall table. "Come on, then. I know just where to take you."

He took her to a place called Patrick Murphy's and introduced her to Mr. Murphy. The man ruffled Sam's hair, kissed her on the cheek and said something that sounded like *the bigger they are, the harder they fall*.

Sam cheeks got pink but he didn't say anything. Mr. Murphy brought them a bottle of wine and suggested the special, chicken parmesan with a side of spaghetti. He smiled broadly when they both promptly closed their menus.

"Anything interesting happen at work today?" Sam asked. He buttered a piece of bread and handed it to her.

"No. Everyone is pretty excited about the awards banquet."

"Monday, right?"

"Yes." She chewed, savoring the mix of sourdough and sweet butter.

He rubbed the cloth napkin between his index finger and thumb. "I don't want to worry you, but I do want you to be really aware of what's going on at the event. Cruz and I haven't been able to put all the pieces together, but there is the possibility that you've been the target all along. If that's true, an event where you're going to be publicly recognized has the potential for danger."

She put down her bread. There would be over two hundred people in attendance. She could not, would not put others in harm's way. "I won't go."

He held up a hand. "No, that's not a good idea. It probably wouldn't make a difference at this point anyway. If the bad guy is tracking you, then he expects you to be there. If you're not, then he might just be pissed enough that he'll do something anyway."

The waiter delivered their plates. It looked delicious, but now she wasn't sure she could eat. "So, there's no good solution?"

"Go. Enjoy. Cruz and I'll both be there as well as other undercover officers. No one is going to be harmed. And maybe we can end this thing." He picked up his fork. "Now, eat. Patrick will be over in a few minutes and you're going to hurt his feelings if you're not a hundred percent vested in enjoying his culinary talents."

She picked up her fork. "I don't want anybody getting hurt because of me. I especially don't want you getting hurt, Sam. I couldn't bear it."

He reached over and snagged her free hand. "Nobody is going to get hurt. I promise."

ON SUNDAY, CLAIRE and Sam slept late. Then they cooked breakfast together. They were just finishing the dishes when Sam's cell phone rang. He listened, said he'd be there in ten minutes and hung up.

"Armed robbery," he said apologetically. "I have to go in. I'm sorry, I wanted to spend the day with you."

"Don't worry. I have to buy a dress for tomorrow night. The only other dress I have is the one I wore when Cruz and I went out."

"You look amazing in that dress, but there's no way, nohow, that you're wearing that dress."

She smiled at him. "Then I have to go shopping."

"I'm not comfortable with you going alone," Sam said.

"I'll see if Hannah is busy." She picked up her cell phone and in minutes had arranged to meet Hannah at the corner of Michigan and Ontario.

"Take a cab," Sam said. "Please."

She nodded and kissed him goodbye.

She found a dress in the third store. It was a dark plum satin. The color flattered her skin tone and there was some simple beading on the full skirt that caught the light, making the dress sparkle when she turned.

"You have to get it," Hannah said.

It was sleeveless, so she bought a smoky-gray wrap for her shoulders. She went to the shoe store next and found strappy sandals that had a heel high enough that she'd be looking most people in the eye.

She was feeling pretty good about herself as she and Hannah hurried down the sidewalk. Five blocks away from Sam's house, Hannah broke off and headed to her apartment. Claire kept walking. It was a gorgeous fall day. She got another block and was waiting for the light to change when she was shoved from behind, right into the path of an oncoming car.

SAM WAS ELBOW-DEEP in paperwork when his desk phone rang. He wanted to ignore it. In addition to the newest case, he and Cruz already had over two dozen open investigations. They didn't need anything else.

He picked it up. "Vernelli," he said.

"Sam, it's Tom Ames. Something's happened."

He was talking fast and Sam's heart started to race. "What's wrong? Is Claire okay?"

"I don't know. I was riding my bike home. I saw a bunch

of emergency lights up ahead and when I got there, I realized it was Claire. She was hit by a car."

His head started to whirl, to conjure up every bad accident scene he'd ever pulled up to. "How badly is she hurt?"

"I don't know. I only got to talk to her for a minute. She said she was okay, but she was already in the ambulance and they seemed to be in a big hurry to get her to United Methodist."

"I'm on my way," Sam said, his heart in his throat.

Chapter Fifteen

Sam hung up, gave Cruz a ten-second explanation and was out of the building in less than a minute. He jumped in his car, put a Mars light on the roof and sped toward the hospital. He'd been a beat cop before he'd made detective. He'd worked hundreds of accident scenes, many involving pedestrians. They were never pretty. Claire could be in bad shape.

Maybe even dying.

He started to shake. He left the car in a no-parking zone and ran into the emergency room. He flashed his badge at the clerk behind the bulletproof glass and motioned for her to buzz him past the locked doors.

Once inside the main emergency area, he ran up to the circular nurses' station and held his badge up again. "Claire Fontaine. Brought in by ambulance. Where is she?"

The nurse checked her computer screen and pointed toward the left. "Room 103. Third down that hallway."

The door was shut.

He paused, his hand raised to knock.

The truth hit him. It didn't matter the extent of her injuries or how scarred she might be. The only thing that mattered was that she was alive.

He wanted her. No matter what. Together they would bear the burden of this day.

He knocked and when the door opened, all he saw was the back of two caregivers bending over Claire, who was lying in a bed. Her clothes were on the floor and they were splattered with blood.

"Claire," he croaked, his throat tight with worry.

Both care providers turned, moving just enough that he could see Claire's face. Her eyes were open.

"How did you get back here?" the doctor said, his tone suggesting that somebody would pay. Wayne Francis, M.D., was stitched across the pocket of his lab coat.

Sam opened his clenched fist and showed his badge for the third time in less than a minute.

"Your questions are going to have to wait, Detective," the doctor said.

Sam ignored the man. He moved into the room, around the doctor and reached for Claire's hand. He held it gently. "Oh, honey, I'm so sorry you're hurt."

"I'm okay," Claire said. "Really."

Sam looked first at the doctor, who had stopped frowning, then at the young nurse in pink scrubs who was smiling. He took that as a good sign and the pressure in his chest started to ease. "How is she?"

The doctor folded his arms across his chest. "I'm getting the impression that this isn't an official visit."

Sam shook his head. It was personal. Real personal. "Claire is my fiancée."

The doctor looked at Claire. "Ms. Fontaine, do I have your permission to discuss your medical condition with this man?"

She nodded.

"Claire is a lucky young woman. She was struck by a midsized sedan and the extent of her injuries appear to be a bloody nose, a sore shoulder and assorted bumps and bruises. Quite frankly, I'm amazed. But as I understand it from the first responder on the scene, she had the common sense to jump before impact, which gave her the momentum she needed to roll up and over the hood of the car."

Claire shrugged and then winced when it apparently bothered her injured shoulder. "I wasn't just the starting pitcher for the Minooka Timberwolves. I ran track, too. Broad jump and pole vaulting. I think both came in handy today."

Sam started to laugh. If anyone had told him fifteen minutes ago that he'd find anything remotely funny about the situation, he'd have set them straight quick. But the look on Claire's face was priceless.

He hated to take it away but he needed facts. "Honey, what happened?"

"I was pushed into traffic."

She said it rather matter-of-fact. Sam's vision started to blur.

"By accident?" he asked, knowing the location was a busy street corner.

She shook her head. "I don't think so. I didn't lose my footing because someone brushed up against me. I tumbled into oncoming traffic because someone pushed me—hard."

Her eyes were bleak. Sam understood. Some of the other things that had happened, she had been able to dismiss as just bad luck or happenstance. This had been a deliberate attempt to hurt her. That knowledge would chill anyone's soul.

"Where was Hannah?" he asked.

"We'd just separated. I know that was stupid. I'm sorry. It was just such a nice day that I didn't think anything bad could happen."

She looked miserable. "It's okay," he reassured her. "You didn't see the person?"

She shook her head. "Street cameras?" she asked.

He nodded. It was just what he'd been thinking. Not only might the camera that covered that intersection have caught something, but she had also been just on the edge of the commercial area. There were still a few businesses and if they were lucky, a couple of them would have had cameras aimed at their entrances. They might be able to piece together where Claire's attacker had come from or escaped to. Maybe even get a vehicle tag.

"Can she go?" Sam asked.

The doctor shook his head. "I'm pretty sure all we're dealing with is a sprained shoulder, but I want her to have an MRI just in case. After that, she's free to go."

"I'm going to make some calls while you do that and then I'll take you home," Sam said.

"Okay." She looked really defeated.

"What's wrong?"

Claire pointed at her things across the room, sitting in a chair. He saw her purse, a shoe box and a cream-colored shopping bag that had tire tracks across it. There were tears in the bag and he could see pieces of material sticking out.

"I must have let go of the bag," Claire said. "The car ran over it. I guess I should be grateful. My face could look like that."

Sam swallowed hard. "But it doesn't. And I don't want you thinking about it."

"The paramedic thought I was a crazy person. I wouldn't get in the ambulance until he gave me the bag. I thought maybe it might just be dirty, but there are rips that can't be fixed." She waved a hand. "It's stupid to be upset about a dress. I'm not going to even think about it."

The doctor stepped forward. "Tammy will take you down for your MRI. Your ride," he said, motioning to a wheelchair in the corner of the room.

She sat up, pulled her thin hospital gown tighter and gracefully transferred over to the wheelchair. Tammy pulled a large plastic bag out of a drawer and gathered up Claire's dirty clothes and shoes. Then she added Claire's purse and the new shoes. She held up the bag with the ruined dress and Claire shook her head. The nurse smiled in return and placed it on the chair.

Claire looked over her shoulder. "Don't wait, Sam. I promise I'll take a cab home after this."

He shook his head. "I'll wait."

After they left the room, the doctor turned toward him. "The aide can pitch that?" he said, motioning to the bag.

Sam shook his head. "I need it."

"Evidence?" the doctor asked.

Sam folded the bag under one arm. "She wants this dress. I'm going to make sure she gets it. I'm going shopping."

The doctor laughed and ran a hand through his gray hair. "Good luck, Detective. You know, they don't teach humility in med school. That said, I have to say, you're a better man than I."

SAM MADE HIS TELEPHONE calls first and got a start on getting a copy of the police report. Then he drove to the dress store. He carried the bag in and carefully pulled the dress out.

The salesclerk, a woman on the downhill side of fifty, reached out and touched the ruined material. "What happened?"

"Long story," Sam said. "I need one just like it."

She looked at the tag. "I'm afraid I just sold our last one a couple hours ago to an absolutely lovely young woman. She had the prettiest brown eyes."

"This is her dress."

"Oh, I am sorry. She was so pretty in it." She paused. "And she didn't need any alterations, which was a blessing because she said she needed it for tomorrow night."

"That's right."

"Well, it is possible that we might have it in another store, but there's no way to get it before then."

"Can you check and see if another store has it?"

There was one in New York. "They're an hour ahead of us," the woman said. "But it's Sunday. There's no way to get it shipped here for delivery tomorrow."

He leaned forward. "Look, I really need the dress. If I can arrange for somebody to be at the store tomorrow morning when they open up, can you arrange for that dress to be waiting for him?"

She cocked her head. "I'm sure I can." She held a hand up to her chest. "You must care a great deal for the young woman."

"I do," he said. As he walked out of the store, he dialed Tom Ames. When he answered, Sam didn't waste any time. He gave him an update on Claire's condition and then said, "I need a favor and I'll make it worth your while."

ONCE THE MRI was finally over, Claire walked out into the exam room, where Sam was waiting. He was the only person in the rather crowded room who wasn't reading a magazine or a book or playing with their phone. He was standing, his back against the wall, his arms folded across his chest, staring at the floor.

He looked up, their eyes met and Claire's heart did a little flutter in her chest. He cared. She could see it, feel it.

"Hi," she said. "They're springing me finally."

He didn't answer, just wrapped an arm gently around her and led her out of the room. He helped her into the car. When she got settled, she turned to him. "I have a prescription for some pain pills," she said. "Could we stop at a pharmacy on the way home?"

"Of course."

That was the only thing he said to her for forty minutes. When they finally parked in the alley behind his house, she turned to him. "Sam, is something wrong?"

He turned to her and his eyes were filled with pain. "I can't stand to see you hurt," he said, his voice rough.

She scooted across the seat and leaned into him. "I'm going to be fine. A couple of days, good as new."

He buried his face in her hair. "It could have ended so much differently," he said, his voice muffled.

"I know," she said. "I know."

They sat in the car, simply holding each other, for another twenty minutes. Finally, Sam lifted his head. "You need to get inside, get some rest."

"I want a shower," she said.

"Okay. Shower first, pain pill second, bed third."

She stood under the hot water for a long time, easing the soreness out of her muscles. When she finally turned off the water, Sam was waiting for her, a big, fluffy towel in hand. He wrapped her in it and gently dried her. Then he led her over to the bed, where he'd already pulled back the covers. There was a glass of water and one of her pain pills on the nightstand.

"I could get used to this," she teased.

"You have my undivided attention," he said as he motioned for her to climb in.

"You're not going back to work?"

"No."

"But—"

He waved a hand. "I'm staying here with you. There's nothing to discuss."

She chewed on her lip, considering. "Okay, but I do have one request."

"Name it," he said.

"Lie down with me," she said. "Please. Just for a little while."

He looked undecided for a moment but then nodded. He sat down and then carefully settled back. He folded his arms underneath his head.

She stared at him. "Not with your clothes on," she said.

He shook his head. "No way, nohow. You're naked. I need to stay fully clothed. Because that's the last thing you need."

"What's the last thing I need?"

He rolled his eyes. "Sex."

She smiled. "You're wrong. But for now, I'll let you off the hook. But I want you to hold me. I want to feel your skin, your warmth. Please."

He shook his head in resignation. "I am putty in your hands." He started taking off his clothes. When he got down to his boxers, he stopped. "Far enough," he proclaimed.

They lay down and she turned onto her uninjured side. He moved in behind her and gently splayed a hand over her hip. "Sleep tight, honey," he said, his voice soft.

She did. When she woke up, the room was dark. Her shoulder ached and she was hungry, but none of that mattered. Sam was still with her.

"How are you feeling?" he whispered.

"Did you sleep?" she asked.

"Oh, yeah."

She was pretty sure he was lying. "What time is it?"

"Almost seven. You've been asleep for a couple hours. I'll go fix you something to eat."

He made her a grilled-cheese sandwich and tomato

soup, which she ate in bed. When he insisted she take a couple of pain pills, she shook her head. "After," she said.

"After what?" he responded.

"After you make love to me." To seal the deal, she used her one good arm to throw back the covers.

His eyes met hers and then very slowly, inch by inch, they traveled down her naked body. She could feel the heat from his body, the intensity of his need.

She spread her legs and he surrendered.

He made love to her, very slowly and very tenderly. There wasn't a place on her that he didn't touch. And then he held her again until morning.

It had made getting shoved in front of a moving vehicle almost worth it.

When the alarm rang, she used her good arm to turn it off. She swung her legs over the side of the bed.

"You could stay home," Sam said.

She shook her head. "I've missed so much time already this week. I have a to-do list that's turning into a 300-pound paperweight."

"Your boss isn't going to give you a hard time about missing work, is he?" Sam asked, sounding very concerned. He sat up in bed.

She cocked her head. "Why? Will you go beat him up if he does?"

Sam nodded. "I'll beat him up and then shoot him. Then I'll start looking for Mission on general principles."

She laughed. "You're too hard on Pete. Although there might not be a whole lot of people standing in your way trying to stop you."

"Why?"

"He's been so irritable. The only good thing is that he's mostly staying in his office. Maybe he's just nervous about the awards ceremony. At least that will be over tonight."

She stood up and gently stretched, completely comfortable being naked in front of Sam.

"Are you nervous?" Sam asked, his eyes on her breasts.

"No. There's no way I'll win. I'm just going to enjoy the experience."

Chapter Sixteen

By the end of the day, Claire's shoulder ached and she was tired of being positive. With her arm in a sling, she had to make some sort of explanation.

She'd soft-pedaled the truth. No sense in blurting out *Someone tried to kill me!* That was a buzz kill. Plus, she didn't have the same trust that she'd had a week ago. All she said was *Wrong place at the wrong time* and *That will teach me to shop.*

She'd just finished clearing her desk when her desk phone rang. She picked it up. "Claire Fontaine."

"I'm downstairs in the lobby," Sam said.

She didn't waste any time. When she reached the lobby, he was standing close to the elevator doors. He looked really irritated.

"What's wrong?" she said.

"I got here a little early and saw the mail guy. I followed him around for a while. I didn't realize that he pushed around a big cart. I figured he carried a bag, sort of like a postal carrier."

Claire shook her head. "We get a lot of sample products coming to us in big boxes. I guess the cart helps."

"He leaves the cart in the hallway when he goes into an office. Anybody could go by and add an envelope to the pile. They wouldn't even have to work in this building."

She got it and understood his frustration. "Well, maybe that makes me feel better. Someone I work with didn't send that note."

"We don't know. Damn it, we just don't know."

She leaned forward and brushed his cheek with a kiss. "Can we forget about it for a little while?"

He looked at her. "I'm sorry. This is your big night. How's the shoulder, by the way?"

"Still there," she said. She started walking fast. "Let's go. We've got only ninety minutes to get ready and get back to the awards ceremony. Victor will have a stroke if I'm late. He's already on edge about Pete. I don't want to be the heavy rock that pulls him over the edge."

"Now what's up with Mission?"

"He left mid-morning. Said he wasn't feeling well. I heard Victor tell him to go home and get some sleep because he expected him to be at tonight's event."

Sam gave her a quick glance. "I spoke to Mission this morning."

"You did? Why?"

"I wanted to know where he was yesterday."

"Was that really necessary?"

He nodded. "Oh, yeah. But he had an alibi that checks out. His dentist has Sunday hours for emergencies. He was there, getting a bad tooth fixed."

"Maybe that's been his problem. Anyway, I knew he wasn't behind this. He's a friend."

Sam held up a hand. "Please. I don't really want to hear how wonderful he is."

She smiled at him. "Or how nice his teeth look?"

"Either."

The afternoon traffic ate up twenty minutes. Claire walked inside Sam's house, dropped her things on the chair in the hallway and said, "I'm going to go take a shower."

She took a fast one and walked into the bedroom wearing just a towel. On the bed was a big white box with a bright blue bow on it.

Sam was standing in the doorway.

"What's that?" she asked.

"It's for you."

She frowned at him. "It's not my birthday."

"That would be so predictable." He took a step into the room.

She felt nervous. Couldn't explain why, but this was the first gift that Sam had given her.

"Allow me," he said with a glance at her arm. He pulled off the lid and set it aside. Then opened the tissue paper.

She felt a ping in the middle of her chest. Her dress. Her beautiful dress. "What?" she asked. She licked her lips. "How?"

He laughed like a little kid at Christmas. "I never thought I'd see you speechless. It makes me feel as if I've finally gotten the upper hand."

"But I took the last dress in my size. I was going to wear one of my work dresses. I figured it would have to do."

"Tom Ames took the red eye to New York LaGuardia. He was waiting at the store when they opened. He had time for a late breakfast in Manhattan before he caught a noon flight back to Chicago."

She could feel her throat closing up. Sam had made all this happen. It was absolutely the nicest thing anyone had ever done for her. She could feel tears gather behind her eyes.

"Oh, no," he said, waving his hands. "No crying. Even happy tears make me fumble around as if I had four thumbs."

She swiped her free hand across her face and smiled the best she could. "I'm living a life of extremes," she said.

"Some really bad stuff. And then there's this. And what we had last night. The most wonderful things. Thank you, Sam. Thank you for everything."

He leaned close and brushed his lips across her cheek. "Put your dress on, pretty girl. We don't want to be late."

THE AWARDS DINNER was at the Minotta Hotel, one of the newest, hippest hotels on Michigan Avenue. The event was on the fortieth floor, in a room that had a wall of windows, allowing attendees to see for miles. It was a dark, clear night and the vastness of Chicago and the surrounding suburbs was a collection of sparkling light.

"Oh, my God," Hannah squealed when she saw Claire. "You're so hot, even with your arm in a sling." The woman turned toward Sam. "And you're not so bad yourself, Detective. Nice tux."

He managed to mumble a thank-you. He'd been pretty much tongue-tied ever since Claire had put on the dress. She was stunning. There was no other word for it.

She truly took his breath away.

"Our table is over here," Hannah said. She led them over to a round table for eight that had a white linen tablecloth, fresh flowers and more forks than he had in his entire house.

Claire's boss, Victor, was there along with his wife on one side and his sister on the other. Marcy wore a skin-tight blue dress that left nothing to the imagination. Her eyes had so much makeup on them that he was surprised she could keep the lids open. Next to her was her date, Terry. He barely looked up from his phone when Victor made introductions.

Hannah sat next to Terry, Claire slid in next to her and then Sam. That left one open seat between him and Victor's wife.

Great. He'd be rubbing elbows with Mission all night.

Better that than letting Mission anywhere near Claire's bare, silky skin. He'd reach for the salt, brush his arm up against Claire and Sam *would* have to kill him.

"I can't imagine Pete would miss this," Hannah said as she helped herself to some fancy stuffed cherry tomatoes offered by a passing waiter. She signaled to a young man twenty feet away who had a tray of chilled shrimp.

"I just talked to him," Victor said, squirming in his chair. "He's on his way."

Good. As distasteful as it would be to sit next to the man, Sam wanted him close. Where he could watch him.

Cruz and two other detectives were already in the room, spread out at three different tables.

Salads had already been delivered and half eaten before Mission arrived. He was pale and he had dark circles under his eyes, making the story that he wasn't feeling well pretty believable. Sam hoped it was his tooth and that the fool wasn't contagious.

Mission nodded in Sam's direction but didn't speak. During dinner, he talked with Victor's wife and answered the occasional question or comment that Hannah volleyed over the table. Dessert had been served and coffee poured when a young woman, wearing a headset, approached the table. She squatted next to Claire but spoke loudly enough to include Mission.

"We need the award finalists up on stage," she said. "You'll be introduced fifth, Mr. Mission, and you'll be the sixth and final introduction, Ms. Fontaine." She motioned for them to stand.

Claire looked longingly at her chocolate mousse.

Sam leaned toward her. "Do you want me to put it in my pocket?" he teased.

She rolled her eyes and pushed back her chair. Mission

got up and stood next to her. Sam expected headset girl to lead them up onto the stage, but instead, she wound her way through the tables until she reached the rear of the room. There were four other people already standing there and Sam assumed they were the other finalists.

He relaxed a little when he saw that Cruz was within twenty feet of the group. But then his heart kicked into high gear when the woman opened a door and ushered the group into the hallway.

He motioned to Cruz to follow them and waited impatiently for Cruz's voice to come through his earpiece.

"Okay here," said Cruz. "The group is backstage. I'll wait outside this door."

Sam tried to calm down. He did not like having Claire out of his sight. The lights on the stage went on and a man wearing a bad-fitting tuxedo walked to the microphone. He introduced himself as the president of the advertising association. He rambled on about the history of the association, the ways the organization supported and educated its membership and finally, the importance of recognizing extraordinary talent.

When he announced that one of the six finalists would take home a $15,000 check, a titter ran through the crowd.

He knew the money would help Claire. She probably didn't make a whole lot and rent was expensive in Chicago. And given that Gregory Fontaine had let it slip that he and Lucille weren't in Claire's financial corner, he'd understood the comments about money that she'd let slip.

He had some money. Had been a good saver for the past ten years. He'd give her whatever she needed.

The screen behind the emcee lit up, flashing a picture of one of the finalists. They read a brief bio and then the screen changed. It was the design entry, a full-page ad, and it was hawking soap.

The same thing happened again and again. Three more finalists, three more products—toothpaste, stainless-steel pans and life insurance. Finally, it was Mission's turn. When his face flashed on the screen, Sam took quiet delight in noting that the man's ears weren't quite level on his head. However, when Mission's design flashed on the screen, Sam did have to admit that it had some appeal. The product was designer shoes. An angel, with flowing gold hair, dressed in a long white gown was sitting on a white cloud in a soft blue sky. The only bright color was her three-inch red heels. Slightly above her, St. Peter was sitting at the entrance of the Pearly Gates looking impatient. The caption above the angel was "I'm not coming without my Binockis."

Then Claire's face came on the screen. It was a good picture. The camera had caught the life in her eyes, the glow of her skin, the sparkle of her smile. Sam had the craziest inclination to stand on his chair, pound his chest and proclaim to the room that *this is my woman.*

Except that would cause Claire to run out onto the stage, grab the microphone and set the record straight.

The screen changed and it was her design. The product was a lawnmower and several blades of grass were discussing the cut in a manner similar to how a woman might discuss her experience at the salon. It was fresh and funny and different than anything he'd ever seen.

He wasn't any great judge of the finer points of an advertising campaign, but he knew what he liked and he thought Mission's and Claire's were the best.

The man on the stage waved his arm. "Let's have a big round of applause to welcome our six finalists to the stage." He announced the first woman's name.

In she walked. She shook hands with the emcee and

took a spot in the first of six circles that had been taped to the stage.

The next finalist was announced and the routine repeated. She took her spot.

It bore a very creepy resemblance to the beauty pageants that he'd seen when he was in junior high and thought it was cool to look at the girls in their swimsuits. He hoped that Claire wasn't going to have to answer a question about how she would make the world a better place.

Finalist three and four were announced. Then, the emcee called for Mission.

After twenty seconds, the crowd started getting restless. Sam lifted his hand and spoke softly into the microphone that was clipped to his shirtsleeve. "Status, Cruz?"

"No activity. What's going on?"

"Mission is AWOL."

The emcee leaned closer to the microphone and spoke in a loud, clear voice. "Pete Mission."

Still nothing.

Something was very, very wrong.

The emcee flipped his paper over. "Claire Fontaine," he said.

There wasn't even a rustle behind the curtain.

They were both missing.

Chapter Seventeen

Sam moved fast. He vaulted up onto the stage, ignoring the other startled contestants. From behind him, he heard one of the officers in the back yell, "Police. Stay in your seats. I repeat, stay in your seats."

He pushed through the heavy curtains into the backstage area. It was dimly lit and empty. He could feel adrenaline whipping through his body and he fought to calm himself down enough to function. Claire's life might depend upon it.

He saw the door on the right that led to the hallway where Cruz still waited. They hadn't gone that direction.

He turned left. It wasn't a large space—there was no place to hide. But then he saw the door. It was really a half door, just wide enough to slip inside. There was no knob, just a spike hammered into the middle of it. *Costumes* was scrawled across it in red paint.

He pulled his gun from his shoulder holster, opened the door and stuck his head around the corner. It was jammed with racks of long dresses on both sides, leaving only a small aisle in the middle.

Claire and Mission were standing at the far end of the room, no more than twelve feet from him. Claire's good arm was wrapped across her body, with the palm resting on her sling. Her lips were pressed together, as if she was very angry. But she didn't look hurt.

Mission had his hands in his pockets and his face was red. He looked miserable.

"Claire?" Sam asked.

"I'm okay, Sam," she said, looking at his gun.

He kept it pointed at Mission. With his other hand, he motioned for her to come to him. When she started toward him, he watched for Mission to make some move to yank her back. But he did nothing.

When Claire got close, he wrapped his free arm around her and pulled her in tight. He sucked in a deep breath, pulling her scent into his lungs. Then he did it again and finally started to feel settled. He lifted his arm and spoke into the wire. "I found both of them. No injuries to report." He brushed his lips across Claire's forehead. "What the hell is going on?"

"Pete had something he needed to tell me," she said.

"And he had to tell you right now?" Sam asked. "There are two hundred people out there waiting for you."

She pressed her lips together. "He stole my design," she said, her tone flat. "I had two ideas and I worked up both of them. In the end, I had to pick one, not realizing that he'd gotten keys from his friend, the super, and broken into my apartment. He wasn't able to access my computer files because I had them password-protected. He saw the hard copies and that was enough for him to copy the idea."

Sam looked at Mission. "You lazy, dishonest son-of-a—"

"I already called him worse," Claire admitted, smiling for the first time. "He had to tell me before I walked out on stage and realized the truth. He didn't trust that I wouldn't blurt something out and the whole world would know."

"You didn't think this through, did you?" Sam asked Mission.

Mission shook his head. "I didn't expect to final. I've entered for over ten years and never been a finalist. I tried to get out of the contest, but Victor wouldn't hear of it. The well was dry. I just needed a little spark."

Sam shook his head and turned toward Claire. "What happens now?"

"Pete and I are going to take our spots on the stage. We're going to get through this night without creating any bigger scene. If Pete wins, he's going to donate the award to charity. Right, Pete?"

Mission nodded.

The urge to beat Mission into a bloody pulp for giving Claire even one moment of distress was pulsating through his veins. The bastard had entered her apartment without permission, had stolen her work, had violated her trust. He needed to pay.

But then Claire turned to him and softly said, "Please, Sam, let me just get through this."

"What's the story you're both going to tell?" Sam asked. "People are going to want to know what caused the delay."

"All we need to say is that Pete wasn't feeling well. Faint, really. Right, Pete?"

He nodded, looking miserable.

"Are you going to tell anybody the truth?"

Mission lifted his head. "I'll tell Victor tomorrow."

At least the jerk was taking some accountability. "Okay, then. Let's get this show on the road," Sam said. He pulled Claire aside and motioned for Mission to precede them out of the narrow room.

Pete caught the emcee's attention. The man hid his annoyance at the delay fairly well, and he got the crowd quieted down. He announced Mission and Pete walked out to his designated circle.

Sam pulled Claire to him and kissed her. It was fast and not nearly enough, but he could not let her walk away without tasting her. "I was scared," he admitted.

She smiled at him. "I didn't think anything shook Sam Vernelli."

Losing her wouldn't just shake him. It would destroy him.

"Claire Fontaine," the emcee announced.

He pulled his arm away. "Go," he said. "They're fools if they don't pick your design to win."

Claire walked onto the stage, took her spot and within minutes, the advertising association proved how smart they were when they announced that Claire was the winner.

The other finalists congratulated her, the emcee handed Claire a check and Claire stepped up to the microphone.

She handled it like a pro. She thanked the association and thanked Victor and her coworkers for the guidance and mentoring that they'd given to her. Then she almost brought him to his knees when she turned slightly, made eye contact with him and said, "It's especially wonderful to have people who are important to me here tonight to share this honor."

He was important to her.

That was good, 'cause he loved her.

Had probably known it for a while, but tonight, when the possibility loomed that she was hurt or missing, he could no longer deny it.

SAM TOOK CLAIRE OUT for a late dinner. They ordered steak and lobster and a bottle of expensive wine. "It's on me," she said, laughing. "I really can't believe it." She picked up her cell phone, which was buzzing. "It's a text from Nadine. I sent her one letting her know that I won."

"What does it say?" he asked, leaning to read it.

"Just 'congratulations'," she said, throwing her phone into her small evening bag.

"What are you going to do with all of it, moneybags?" Sam asked. "Bury it in the backyard?"

"I don't have a backyard, but I don't intend to carry it around. I'll take it to the bank tomorrow. It's nice knowing I've got a little breathing room. I'll sleep better now." Her cheeks turned pink. "Not that I haven't slept pretty good the last several nights."

They hadn't done all that much sleeping. "Me, too," he said. "Although I'd sleep better if we'd been able to find the connection between you and Sandy Bird."

"I know. Maybe there is no connection. The burglary. Sandy Bird. The horrible phone message. That stupid note at work. Maybe they were all just a series of random events."

"I don't think so. Don't let your guard down. Stay watchful."

She leaned toward him and whispered in his ear, "How about you watch me. I'm going to…"

He listened. And his heart rate sped up. He signaled for the bill. "Tell me again," he said.

THE NEXT MORNING, Sam waited outside his house for Cruz. He'd asked his partner for a ride to work after Tom Ames had asked to borrow his SUV to drive his mother to see her parents. The young man said he wasn't sure his mother's old car would make it.

Sam was happy enough to loan the vehicle. He owed Tom. Detectives were required to use squad cars during the day. He and Cruz usually drove separately to the pickup lot, but he'd called Cruz earlier that morning and asked him to swing by.

Cruz being Cruz was ten minutes late. Sam was just about to call him on his cell phone when his friend pulled up in his gray Toyota. Sam opened the door and had to pick up a to-go container off the seat before he could sit down.

"What the hell was that?" he asked, tossing it over his shoulder.

Cruz drove with one hand and patted his stomach with the other. "Biscuits and gravy, topped with sunny-side up eggs."

Sam frowned at his partner. "Have you *had* your cholesterol checked lately?"

Cruz kept his eyes on the road. "It's just numbers."

"Numbers that will kill you."

Cruz sighed. "Let me know when we're done with today's public service announcement."

Sam didn't respond.

Finally, Cruz turned toward him. "I got a call from Franco this morning. He's been asking around about pawnshop girl and he said she's dropped off the face of the earth. Some of his friends are real disappointed because she sold good drugs at a reasonable price."

Sam clenched his fists so tight that his fingers hurt. "Electronics are stolen and then pawned by someone who deals. Then a nice suburban woman randomly picks the same apartment to break into and threatens to kill the occupants. Then Claire gets a call from some idiot where the man clearly knows information about a confidential police investigation. Then there's the note Claire gets at work. No wonder we can't make any progress. None of it makes any sense."

"Maybe we're adding two and two together and coming up with five," Cruz said.

"This isn't algebra," Sam said, barely able to keep his temper.

Cruz looked over and studied him. "Maybe not, Sam. But it is a puzzle and it's our job to put the pieces together."

"I know what my job is." He stared out the window, seeing but not really seeing the passing streets. Everywhere he looked, people walked and talked on their cell phones and sipped big cups of coffee. As if they didn't have a care in the world.

He watched two young punks, neither a day over sixteen, saunter up the street, hands in their jacket pockets. The two of them went into the coffee shop on the corner.

Hell. What kind of worries could they have if they could afford a four-dollar cup of coffee?

He and Cruz were almost past the shop, almost past the big front window when he saw it. If he hadn't been looking, if the sun hadn't been shining just right through the plate glass, he'd have never seen the man behind the counter, his hands in the air, or the boy-turned-perp, his arm waving wildly around, a gun in his hand.

"Stop." He pointed toward the curb with one hand, reached automatically for the radio, and came up empty. He yanked his cell phone out of his suit coat pocket and dialed 9-1-1.

When the phone was answered he didn't waste any time. "This is Detective Sam Vernelli, Area 5, Violent Crimes. We've got an armed robbery in progress at the Tasty Mill—it's a coffee shop at the corner of Houston and Applewood. My partner and I are going in. We need backup, no lights or sirens. No pass-by." He didn't want the creeps looking up, seeing a blue-and-white go by and freaking out. He waited just long enough for the operator to read back the location and he hung up.

Cruz pulled into an empty space and they were out of

the car and moving fast. They stayed close to the building. Sam knew that even if one of the perps was doing lookout, he wouldn't be able to see them unless he stuck his head out the door. "I'll take the back," Cruz said. "I've been in this place. Door opens into a hallway with a couple of restrooms. Right past them is the dining room. Give me forty seconds," Cruz said and started running for the back door.

Sam edged forward, his back against the brick wall. Counting. When he got to thirty-five, he raised his gun. At thirty-eight, he swung his body around. At forty, he was going through the door.

Cruz exploded from the back at exactly the same time. "Police. Drop your weapons," Sam yelled. "Now!"

Chapter Eighteen

The Hispanic boy on the right, looking like he was about to piss his pants, let his gun fall to the hardwood floor. Sam thought it was a damn miracle that it didn't go off. The Caucasian kid, maybe a year or two older, kept his gun pointed at the store clerk. His arm was shaking and sweat poured off his face.

"Don't be an idiot," Sam said. "Put your gun down. Now!"

It was five long seconds before the kid did so.

His gun leveled at the kids' chests, Sam moved close enough to kick their weapons far out of reach.

"Get on the floor," Cruz ordered. "Get your face on the floor."

Both boys obeyed. Sam sucked in a breath. It had gone well.

Then he heard a noise and he looked over his shoulder just in time to see a young woman in the corner, back by the napkins and spoons, point a gun at Cruz.

The bullet hit Cruz's upper thigh. His whole body jerked back and he stumbled into a stand-up rack of greeting cards, taking them with him when he fell to the ground.

Sam swung his gun around to return fire, but the girl dropped her weapon, put her hand over her mouth and sank to her knees. Sam, his heart about to burst, kept his gun on the two young men at the front of the store while he circled behind her.

Then there were cops pouring in the door. EMTs came next and they moved quickly to get a still-conscious Cruz into the waiting ambulance.

Sam grabbed his partner's hand as they wheeled him past. It scared the hell out of him when the man's grip was weak. He'd lost so much blood. "Hang in there, Cruz," he urged.

"They. Keep. Getting. Younger," Cruz said, his words coming in spurts.

Cruz was right. The girl couldn't have been much over fourteen. And she'd come this close to killing his partner.

It could have been him.

Next time it might be.

"I'll come as soon as I can," Sam promised his friend as they loaded Cruz in the ambulance.

"If I don't make it," Cruz said, his voice faint, "take care of Meg. Make sure she's okay."

Sam nodded and slammed the doors of the ambulance shut. He pulled his cell phone out of his pocket and dialed Meg's cell number. He'd memorized it years ago in the event something horrible like this ever happened. And when she answered, he quickly realized that she'd spent those same years preparing for just such a call. She was calm, decisive and said she would catch the next plane to Chicago.

Then he called Claire. Didn't stop to think why. Just knew that he needed to hear her voice. He told her what happened, assured her that he was okay and promised to call her with any news.

Sam knew it would take a while to sort out the red tape. Police incidents where weapons were discharged, especially when the perps were minors, were getting front-page news coverage. Every detail would be under scrutiny.

While neither he nor Cruz had discharged their own weapon, which would have required a roundtable meeting, a cop had been shot. Other cops took that real seriously. Sam knew he wasn't going anywhere until he'd given his statement. He knew other detectives had been dispatched to the hospital to get Cruz's story.

He and Cruz wouldn't be allowed to speak until that had happened. There could be no room for doubt at the conclusion of the investigation that statements had been given independently.

The press would be all over this. They'd spin it and analyze it and radio talk-show hosts would pick up the story if it were a slow news day. Sam didn't like it but he understood it. After all, he'd been close to being on the other side of the desk.

When he finally got the free-to-go nod from his captain, he drove like a maniac to the hospital. Captain Morris had given him an update an hour earlier, had said that Cruz was getting patched up in the Emergency Room. Sam knew he wouldn't rest until he actually saw Cruz.

He parked and showed his badge to get quickly past the hospital security. He asked for the charge nurse and when he told her why he was there, it didn't take him long to realize that everything wasn't fine, that everything might not be fine.

From far away, he heard her say things like blood clot, possible stroke, in surgery at this very minute. He let her lead him to the other side of the hospital, to a mostly empty waiting room. Claire was the only person there.

"You didn't need to come," he said, wrapping his arms around her and holding her gently, being careful of her sore shoulder.

"I know how much he means to you, Sam. I didn't want you to be alone."

He took the comfort that she so freely gave. When his legs finally felt like they might just keep him up, he pulled back far enough that he could see her face.

"I'm so glad it wasn't you, Sam. I'm so glad you weren't hurt."

"I was scared, Claire." He pulled her close and rested his chin on the top of her head. "I was so scared. I almost shot that girl."

She wrapped her free arm around him like before and held him tight. "What happened?" she asked, her words muffled by his chest.

"She was the inside guy. She had a cell phone and she'd called her friends and told them to come, that the store was almost empty. I'm not even sure those boys knew she had a gun. They just froze when she shot Cruz. I really don't think they were planning on shooting anybody."

A woman, in her early forties, walked into the room. She had on green scrubs and her hair was pulled back and covered by a hairnet. "I'm Dr. Janssen. I understand you're his partner. We got the bleeding stopped, replaced two pints of blood and got him stabilized. He's in the recovery room now. I'll be back in a few minutes and take you to see him."

The woman, her rubber-soled clogs softly clumping, left the room. Sam sat in his chair and tried to remember all the bargains he'd made with God when he'd seen Cruz bleeding out on the coffee-shop floor. He intended to keep every one of them.

"He might not be happy that I called Meg."

"That was the right thing to do," she said. "I would want somebody to call me."

That would be horrible. My God, he'd been just three

years younger than she was now when he'd walked in and practically stumbled over Tessa's dead body.

The doctor returned. "Mrs. Vernelli can come, too," she said.

Mrs. Vernelli.

Tessa had spent hours writing that on all her notebooks. When he'd introduced her to friends as Tessa Fontaine, she'd put out her hand, flashed a smile and said, "You can call me Mrs. Vernelli."

She was crazy about being Mrs. Vernelli.

They'd been kids playing grown-up games.

Now he was a grown-up acting like a kid. He'd met Claire, seen something he wanted and regardless of the consequences, had decided he had to have it.

She was a young, beautiful woman. She'd been protected her whole life, sheltered, almost shut away. She'd been lonely.

This was her time to soar. The sky was the limit for Claire Fontaine.

Unless she was tied to some idiot who could get shot at most any day. Then she'd just be a young widow. Alone and lonely again.

"She's not Mrs. Vernelli," he said, his voice hard.

Claire's head snapped up.

He looked at her and prayed that he'd have the courage to keep going. "You were right, Claire. It was a crazy idea to pretend we were getting married, to even think about it. Call your parents. Make sure they understand that it's over."

"You want it to be over?" she asked, her voice choked with tension. "Everything?"

"Yeah. I don't know what the hell I was doing."

"Is it because of Tessa?" she asked.

He nodded. It was better for her to think so. Better

for her to believe he was trapped by the past rather than afraid of the future. Maybe this was the one last thing he could do for her.

With a careless swipe of her hand, she brushed a tear off her cheek. "I'm sorry she died, Sam. I loved her, too. I'd like to think that she would have wanted us both to be happy."

"Detective Vernelli?" The doctor still stood in the doorway, looking very impatient.

Claire glanced from him to the doctor, then back to him. Her eyes were bright with tears. "He's right. I'm not Mrs. Vernelli." She stood on her tiptoes and kissed his cheek. "Goodbye, Sam."

CRUZ WAS FLAT ON HIS BACK in a bed, with an IV pumping something into his arm. He was pale and his mouth was a tight line. His eyes were closed.

Sam closed his own eyes and said a quick prayer. Then he opened them and gave a low whistle. "Some people will do *anything* for a couple weeks off," he said.

Cruz opened his eyes and wet his dry lips with his tongue. "It would have been a better plan if they'd shot you and I took off time to take care of you."

Sam sat down in the lone chair, extended his legs and crossed them at the ankles. "Doc says you're going to be fine."

Cruz nodded. "She said if I work like hell in physical therapy, I should get full use back."

Sam let out the breath that he must have been holding. "I assume you gave your statement."

"Yeah. Right after I got here. I was fine for the first hour and then all hell broke loose."

"What? You weren't getting enough attention?"

"I've had my fair share now," Cruz said, his voice

sounding strained. Sam knew he shouldn't stay much longer. His friend would need sleep.

"I called Meg," Sam said. "I hope you're not mad. She's coming."

"I don't want her pity," Cruz said.

"Give her a chance," Sam cautioned. "She—"

He stopped when a nurse entered the room. She smiled, walked over and checked the machines that were beeping and whirling and left, her clogs making the same soft noise he'd heard earlier when the doctor had walked through the waiting area. She had on a similar purple-and-green smock.

She was a walking color wheel. Whatever happened to the white uniform, little white hat and ugly white shoes?

Sam stood up, leaned over Cruz's bed to tell his friend goodbye and stopped.

No white shoes. Green clogs. Just like the green clogs that had been under Claire's kitchen table the day Sandy Bird had stormed her way in.

Oh, damn.

"Sam?" Cruz said, his voice full of fear. "What the hell's wrong? Am I bleeding somewhere?"

"No. No." Sam rushed to assure his friend. "Cruz, I think I missed something. Something big. That nurse that was just in here. She had on green clogs. The doctor did, too. Nadine, Claire's roommate, works at this hospital and she wears them."

"Maybe it's the pain medication, Sam, but you're not making a lot of sense."

"The day of the shooting, I moved Nadine and Claire into the kitchen. Claire almost tripped over the shoes, so I kicked them under the table. And now, I remember that when I got behind Nadine and I told her to put her gun down, her feet were bare. She laid her gun next to bare feet."

"So? She'd taken her shoes off."

"No. She said she'd been leaving for work when Sandy Bird, a stranger, had surprised her in the hall. That she pushed her way into the apartment. Claire heard them arguing in the living room. I don't think Nadine took the time to take her shoes off and put them in the kitchen when she's got a stranger waving a gun in her face."

"She invited her in," Cruz said, coming to the logical conclusion. "She knew her."

Sam rubbed a hand over his face. "I don't know how. I thought we'd looked at every possible connection. All I know is that her shoes were under the table."

Cruz lifted his head up off the bed, just inches. "Call The Weasel. If they were there, he'd have gotten a picture of them."

Sam hit the door running. "I'll be back," he said over his shoulder.

"I NEED THE WEASEL," he said, when the department phone was answered.

In less than a minute, the man was on the phone. "What's up, Vernelli?"

"About three weeks ago you worked the scene at 810 Maple Street. Head shot, hardwood floor."

"Ah, yes, I remember it well. Did they ever get that wall clean?"

"I need to see the pictures. All of them. I'm on my way in. I'll meet you at my desk in fifteen minutes."

The Weasel was waiting for him when he got there. It took Sam less than three minutes to find the photo he wanted. There they were. Ugly green clogs. Under Claire and Nadine's table.

It was starting to make sense. After Claire had surprised the two of them, things had turned bad quickly. Bird hadn't been a stranger. She hadn't come for Claire. She'd come to see Nadine.

Sam picked up his cell phone and started to dial Claire's cell number. He stopped, suddenly shaking so hard that he couldn't press the small buttons on his phone. The call had come into Claire's home telephone.

The caller was somebody who knew that new number.

Like maybe the roommate who'd been there when the telephone line got activated. It had been a man who called. But something told him that Nadine Myer was in this up to her eyebrows. She'd grown up with Claire, their families knew each other. She would know about Tessa.

He and Nadine were going to have a little conversation.

For the second time that day, Sam got in his car and drove like a crazy man to Melrey Hospital. He went to the front desk this time and asked to see the administrator in charge.

In less than two minutes, a middle-aged woman, wearing a white lab coat and the same awful shoes walked toward him. "Detective, I'm Margaret Moore, Director of Nursing. May I help you?"

He pulled out a card. "I'm investigating a potential homicide. I need to speak with one of your employees. Ms. Nadine Myer. I'm going to need someplace private."

"I'm afraid I can't help you. Nadine Myer hasn't worked here for six weeks. Trust me on this, Detective. Nadine won't ever work at this hospital again."

Sam started to get a bad feeling. "Why not?" he asked.

Margaret Moore looked around. The lobby was full of people. "Follow me," she said.

Chapter Nineteen

Claire knew she should go back to work but she just couldn't bear it. Instead, she went to her apartment. She could barely put one foot in front of the other as she made her way up the three flights of stairs. She was grateful that Nadine was working. She couldn't face anybody.

She went to her bedroom and sat on her bed. She'd have to leave Chicago after all. Then she wouldn't have to worry about running into Sam or Sam stopping by to check on her ever again.

She wouldn't go back to Nebraska. Maybe New York. There were advertising agencies there. Maybe they'd be willing to take a chance on somebody new. At least she had the award that she could add to her résumé. And some seed money. The check was really going to come in handy now. She knew rent would be even more in New York than it had been in Chicago and she wouldn't have anyone to share the expense with. She couldn't expect Nadine to leave a good job in Chicago just because Claire's life was falling apart.

She would need to give notice to Alexander and Pope. She should do that today. She got up, opened her desk drawer and searched for her nice lined paper. She found the paper but realized that something else was missing.

Her passport.

She always kept it in this drawer. She'd seen it in there just a few weeks ago. She slipped off the sling so that she'd have use of both arms. She yanked out the drawer and dumped the contents on her bed. She rummaged through the items and came up empty.

They'd been robbed again.

How was that possible? Feeling ill, she walked into Nadine's room to see what might have been taken from there. Two minutes later, she tried to open Nadine's closet doors but realized the folding door was caught on a suitcase. She pulled the bag out with some difficulty because it was heavy. What the heck?

She opened it. It was jammed full of clothes, almost everything Nadine had in her closet. Lying on top was a short, dark-haired wig, styled almost exactly how Claire wore her hair.

She started to feel sick. The woman who'd pawned the stolen items had had short, dark hair.

And she realized there never had been a robbery. It had been Nadine.

She was sitting there on the floor, holding the horrible wig in her hands, when she heard her front door open. She threw the wig back into the suitcase, closed it, pushed it back in the closet and ran for the door.

But Nadine was already inside.

She looked at Claire and then past her into Claire's bedroom where the contents of her middle drawer still lay spread across her bed. Before Claire could even move, Nadine pulled her gun out of her purse.

"I didn't expect you to be here until tonight," Nadine said, her tone angry. "But I guess I can get an early start."

"Start?" Claire asked.

"I'm leaving the country. That wig and your passport are going to come in handy."

"Nadine," Claire said, trying not to choke on the tears that threatened. She was so scared. "It doesn't have to be this way. We can talk about it." She needed to buy enough time to get the gun away from Nadine.

"Talk?" Nadine shook her head. "I'm in this so deep and that damn boyfriend of yours isn't going to ever let it go. I don't have time to talk." She waved her gun around and Claire's stomach jumped. Nadine walked over and dumped the contents of Claire's purse onto the bed. The award check floated out.

"Excellent," Nadine said. "This is what I was hanging around for. Now, come on. We're getting out of here. Move or I'll shoot you now."

Claire knew she wasn't kidding. Nadine had already killed once and she would do it again.

"Where are we going?" Claire asked.

"Shut up," Nadine said. "Get my suitcase. Come on, move."

Claire picked up the heavy case and set it by the door. "No, you carry it," Nadine said. "We're going to walk out that door and down to my car."

Claire opened the door just as the phone in the apartment started ringing. Nadine pulled the door shut behind them. Their neighbor was just coming back from somewhere. The woman turned and looked at them, then at the suitcase.

"You two girls going on a trip?" she asked.

Claire heard Nadine suck in a breath. "Yes," Claire said, forcing herself to sound normal. "To Saint Louis. Big game between the Cubs and the Cards."

MARGARET MOORE LED SAM down to a small, windowless office. She cleared off a chair so that he could sit. "Nadine was discharged from our employ. She's not welcome on the premises."

"What did she do to get fired?"

"Theft. Narcotics. Are you familiar with fentanyl, Detective Vernelli?"

On the street pure fentanyl was a big-time favorite with addicts. "Some."

"Well, in the operating room, it's used a great deal. However, we realized that we were missing a fairly large quantity. As part of our investigation, we asked Ms. Myer to take a drug test. She refused and we terminated her."

"Could it possibly have been anyone else?"

"No. Our investigation proved that it was her. We do know she had some help. Not that you may be interested, but we fired a pharmacist that same day. He admitted that he'd helped her. We're also short significant amounts of Oxycontin. Evidently, they had some kind of relationship, although I believe it was short-lived."

Relationship with a pharmacist. He needed to pay Fletcher Bird another visit.

But first, he needed to get Claire away from Nadine.

"Thank you," he said. "You've been very helpful."

"Detective Vernelli," she said, stopping him, "if it helps, I think she fooled a lot of people. We never had any indication that she was impaired."

He'd worked with several functioning alcoholics and addicts, too. People got good at hiding the addiction. All he knew was that she was going to pay for giving Claire even one moment of grief. He left the office, dialing his cell phone as he walked. He slammed it shut when Claire's cell line rang and rang until it switched over to voice mail. "Call me, Claire. Right now," he said. He ended the call and fumbled in his wallet for the card that had her office number. He dialed it. The receptionist answered and said that Claire hadn't been in the office for several hours.

Next, he called the landline at her apartment. It rang and rang. He squeezed the steering wheel and tried to think.

She'd been upset when she'd left the hospital. If she hadn't gone back to work, where would she have gone? To his house? No. Shopping? He didn't think so.

It only made sense that she'd have gone home. Maybe she was sleeping and couldn't hear the phone? Maybe she heard it and didn't intend to ever talk to him again?

Please, please, just be safe.

With few other options, he drove to her apartment building and ran up the three flights of stairs. He pounded on the door.

The neighbor from across the hall stuck her head out the door. "Keep it down," she snarled. "I'm watching my shows."

"I'm looking for Claire. Have you seen her?"

"Yeah. She left about five minutes ago. Both her and Nadine."

"Did she say anything?"

"Yeah. Said they were going to Saint Louis to see the Cubs play."

That didn't make any sense. The season had been over for three weeks.

But Nadine probably didn't know that. Claire had been trying to let someone know that there was something wrong.

Sam pulled out his cell and called his captain next. He needed help.

IT WAS THE SECOND TIME Claire had seen Nadine's gun. It was the first time it had been pointed at her. Nadine held it in her lap, the short, black barrel pointed upward at a forty-five-degree angle, directly at Claire's head.

She wished she could assume that Nadine wasn't desperate enough to shoot her when she had control of the wheel. But she knew she couldn't really assume anything about Nadine.

So while she should have been terrified, she was really just numb. The woman who'd been her friend, her very best friend for years, had lied to her many times over.

"I think I deserve to know why," she said.

"Just start the damn car," Nadine ordered.

Claire turned the ignition key. Nadine reached for the heat control and turned it on high. Neither of them had on coats and the air was cold.

"Drive," Nadine said, bringing the gun an inch closer.

Claire checked her side mirror and pulled out.

"That way!" Nadine waved her hand, pointing to a street on Claire's right.

"I thought you needed to go to the airport."

Nadine didn't answer her and Claire knew the truth. She wasn't ever going to see the airport. Nadine wasn't intending to let her live that long.

She turned as directed, buying time. "Well?" she prompted.

Nadine turned to her, her normally pretty face red with anger. "My daddy isn't rich like your daddy. He doesn't have five or six companies. When I met Bobby—"

"Bobby?" Claire interrupted. "Who's Bobby?"

"He's a pharmacist. He made good money and had figured out a way to supplement his income. Between the two of us, we were able to take a lot of drugs. We used some and sold the rest to people who were willing to pay a whole lot of money for what we had." She smiled, but it didn't reach her eyes. "We were a good team."

"What went wrong, Nadine?" She slowed the car down a couple miles per hour and prayed Nadine wouldn't notice.

"I got fired."

"Why?"

"Because Bobby couldn't keep his numbers straight and they figured out that there were drugs missing. He got fired, too. So we were both out of a job with no hope of finding another one. Melrey had reported me to the state and my license was suspended."

"Why didn't you just tell me?" Claire asked. "I would have helped."

"I don't need any handouts from my rich friend. I found a way. I met Sandy Bird at the gambling boat. She was bragging about her husband, the pharmacist. The joke was on her because in less than two weeks he was sleeping with me. But he was so stupid. I only had to do it twice before I told him that I was going to tell his wife if he didn't get me what I needed."

Claire saw a group of construction workers on the side of the road. She deliberately let her eyes rest on the men. Distracted, Nadine looked, too. "Don't even think about it," she warned. She leaned over just far enough to jab the gun into Claire's side.

Claire kept driving, praying Nadine wouldn't realize that in the second she'd looked away, Claire had turned on her emergency flashers. The soft clicks reverberated in her ears but with the heat billowing, she didn't think Nadine could hear the noise. They drove for several more minutes, leaving behind the residential area and entering a run-down industrial area filled with one-story, tin-sided buildings that appeared deserted.

"So you pretended we were robbed so that you could hock my things."

"I needed money. I knew your daddy could buy you more."

"You killed Sandy Bird."

"I had to. How was I to know that Fletcher would be stupid enough to tell his wife about us? I don't know why she cared that he was sleeping around—he was a dud in bed. But she obviously was pissed. I couldn't be sure she wasn't going to shoot us. And if she didn't, I figured it wasn't going to be long before she said something that would make you realize she wasn't some stranger."

"But it didn't stop there?" Claire asked.

"No." Nadine waved her gun. "Pull in here."

It was a gravel-and-dirt alley, flanked on both sides by gray, windowless, metal buildings. "Get out," Nadine ordered. Once they were both out of the vehicle, she motioned for Claire to keep walking. She had her gun pointed at Claire's back.

"You're never going to get away with this," Claire said, her throat almost closing up with fear. She'd been so sure that someone would see her, would help her. But now it was just her and Nadine. "Sam will figure it out."

"If you hadn't involved him," Nadine said, her tone hard, "none of this would have happened. He had to keep trying to figure it out, asking questions, making people nervous. I had been so careful—never calling Fletcher at home or at work, never going to see him there. But I couldn't be sure that at some point, if somebody kept digging hard enough, they wouldn't find a connection between the two of us. Sam Vernelli was ruining everything."

"You made that call, the one about Tessa."

Nadine swiped the back of her hand across her face. She was sweating. "I bought a homeless guy a steak dinner. That's all it took to make sure your cop friend thought everything was connected to your sister's murder."

Claire swallowed hard and prayed that she wouldn't throw up. "I guess you probably wrote the note I got at work, too."

"I thought it was a nice touch," Nadine said, her tone sarcastic. "In there," she instructed. She waved her gun at a long, one-story cement-and-metal structure that was missing part of the roof and most of its windows. She pushed Claire toward it. Claire stumbled, catching herself on one knee. She took her time in getting up. She would not go inside that building. If Nadine wanted to kill her, she'd have to do it outside.

Claire stopped walking.

"Move," Nadine screamed.

Claire turned and let loose with the ball of wet dirt and gravel that she'd picked up. It hit Nadine in the face just as Claire threw her body at the woman.

They rolled in the dirt, legs kicking, arms flailing.

Claire had the advantage of strength and surprise. And it didn't matter that she had only one really good arm.

She had Nadine flat on her back, sitting on her stomach, when the first squad car pulled into the alley.

Sam's car was thirty seconds behind. He ran toward her, pulled her tight into his body and rocked her in his strong arms.

He shook so hard that it seemed like the ground was trembling. "Oh, Claire, sweetheart," he said. He pulled back just enough to look at her face. "Are you hurt?"

She was covered with dirt and her blouse was torn, but all in all, she felt pretty darn good. She sucked in a deep breath. Life was wonderful.

"How did you know we were here?" she asked.

"A beat cop doing regular patrol happened to see you go by. Saw your hazard lights on and it made him take a second look at the car. He called it in and—" Sam stopped

"—and I prayed all the way here that we wouldn't be too late."

"You made it," she said.

He shook his head, looking dazed. "You didn't even need us. What happened?"

"I threw a pretty nice curve ball."

He grabbed her again and held her tight. "Oh, God, Claire. I've been a fool. Please, please, say you'll marry me. I can't live without you. I love you so much."

They were the words she'd been waiting for.

But she had to ask the question that would not be denied.

"What about Tessa?"

He held her face between his hands. Gently. Lovingly. "I loved your sister. I loved her with the passion of a young man. And for some crazy reason, I felt disloyal to her memory when I started to fall for you. I felt guilty because I was so happy and she was never going to get the chance for that kind of happiness."

"What changed?"

"When I had to go back through that investigation file, it forced me to really think about Tessa. And to remember her. All her strengths, all her faults. But what I really remembered was that Tessa lived life to its fullest. Every day was a party for her, every day was an adventure. She was the type that would have expected me to keep living. She'd have wanted me to love again."

"But at the hospital?"

"I was being stupid. I said that it would never work because I was scared. Scared that something could happen to me and that you'd be left alone. I didn't want you to ever have to be lonely again."

"That could still happen," she said.

"I know, but I'm not going to make the mistake that

your parents made. I'm not going to be afraid to love or be afraid to have someone love me. Being afraid of love, just because you might get hurt, is a waste of a life. I won't do it. That's the legacy Tessa left us. She taught us to live."

Claire put her hand on his arm. "We're no closer to knowing who killed Tessa."

Sam nodded. "We may never know."

"Are you okay with that?"

"For her, I want to know. For her, I want justice served. But what I couldn't accept is falling short of being the kind of man she'd have wanted her little sister to marry."

The starting pitcher of the Minooka Timberwolves smiled. "I think she'd be happy for us."

"I know she would be. Let's go home."

* * * * *

Next month, Beverly Long's THE DETECTIVES
continues with Cruz Montoya's story.
Look for SECURE LOCATION
wherever Harlequin Intrigue books are sold!

COMING NEXT MONTH from Harlequin® Intrigue®
AVAILABLE MARCH 19, 2013

#1413 CARDWELL RANCH TRESPASSER
B.J. Daniels

A stranger has entered Cardwell Ranch, and Hilde Jacobson is the only person who can see her for who she really is. Risking her own life—and heart—she joins forces with the only man she can trust, Deputy Marshal Colt Dawson.

#1414 SCENE OF THE CRIME: DEADMAN'S BLUFF
Carla Cassidy

When FBI agent Seth Hawkins takes a vacation the last thing he expects while riding some sand dunes is to find a live woman buried in the sand.

#1415 CONCEAL, PROTECT
Brothers in Arms: Fully Engaged
Carol Ericson

When Noelle Dupree escapes Washington, D.C., for some peace and solitude at her Colorado ranch, danger follows her. Can a sexy cowboy ease her fears, or will he bring mayhem to her doorstep...and her heart?

#1416 STAR WITNESS
The Delancey Dynasty
Mallory Kane

If Harte and Dani can trust each other enough to survive a killer storm and a deadly chase, one night will be enough to forge a lasting love.

#1417 ROYAL RESCUE
Royal Bodyguards
Lisa Childs

For three years FBI agent Brendan O'Hannigan thought Josie Jessup dead. To keep both her and the son he didn't know about alive, he'll willingly give up his own life.

#1418 SECURE LOCATION
The Detectives
Beverly Long

Detective Cruz Montoya has one chance to save his ex-wife and their unborn child...but will old secrets get in the way?

You can find more information on upcoming Harlequin® titles, free excerpts and more at www.Harlequin.com.

HICNM0313

Colt saw that she had a stunned look on her face. Stunned and disappointed. It was heartbreaking.

Without a word, he took her in his arms. Hilde was trembling. He took her over to the couch, then went to her liquor cabinet and found some bourbon. He poured her a couple fingers worth.

"Drink this," he said.

"Aren't you afraid what I might do liquored up?" she asked sarcastically.

"Terrified," he said, and stood over her until she'd downed every drop. "You want to talk about it?" he asked, taking the empty glass from her and joining her on the couch.

She let out a laugh. "*I* hardly believe what happened. Why would I expect anyone else to?"

"I believe you. I believe everything you've told me."

Tears welled in her brown eyes. He drew her to him and kissed her, holding her tightly. "I'm sorry you had to go through this alone."

She nodded and wiped hastily at the tears as she drew back to look at him. "You're my only hope right now. We have to find out everything we can about this woman." And then she told him everything, from finding the shop vandalized to what led up to her being nearly arrested.

When she finished, he said, "We shouldn't be surprised."

"Surprised? I'm still in shock. To do something like that to yourself…"

"You knew Dee was sick."

Hilde nodded. "What will she do next? That's what worries me."

Colt didn't want to say it, but that's what worried him. "Maybe Hud has the right idea. Isn't there somewhere—"

"I'm not leaving. Dee told me that I've never had to fight for anything. Well, I'm fighting now. I'm bringing her down. One way or another."

"Hilde—"

"She has to be stopped."

"I agree. But we have to be careful. She's dangerous." He felt his phone vibrate, checked it and saw that his boss had sent him a text. "Hud wants to see me ASAP." Not good. "I don't want to leave you here alone."

"I'll be fine. Dee won this round. She won't do anything for a while and I'm not going to give her another chance to use me like she did today."

He heard the courage, as well as the determination, in her voice. Hilde was strong and, no matter what Dee had told her, she *was* a fighter.

*Can Hilde and Colt stop Dee's deadly plan
before it's too late?*

*Find out what happens next in
CARDWELL RANCH TRESPASSER. Available March 19
from Harlequin Intrigue!*

It all starts with a kiss

Check out the brand-new series

HARLEQUIN KISS™

Fun, flirty and sensual romances.
ON SALE JANUARY 22!

Visit www.tryHarlequinKISS.com
and fall in love with
Harlequin® KISS™ today!